TELL
ME
ANOTHER
STORY

—

Puffin Books

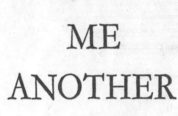

PUFFIN BOOKS

Published by the Penguin Group
27 Wrights Lane, London W8 5TZ, England
Viking Penguin Inc., 40 West 23rd Street, New York, New York 10010, USA
Penguin Books Australia Ltd, Ringwood, Victoria, Australia
Penguin Books Canada Ltd, 2801 John Street, Markham, Ontario, Canada L3R 1B4
Penguin Books (NZ) Ltd, 182–190 Wairau Road, Auckland 10, New Zealand

Penguin Books Ltd, Registered Offices: Harmondsworth, Middlesex, England

First published 1964
30 29 28 27 26 25 24 23

Made and printed in Great Britain by
BPCC Hazell Books Ltd
Member of BPCC Ltd
Aylesbury, Bucks, England
Set in Linotype Granjon

Contents

Acknowledgements

Grateful acknowledgements are due to the following:

A. & C. Black Ltd and Clive Sansom for 'The Airman' from *Speech Rhymes*; Bodley Head Ltd for 'The Stamping Elephant' from *A Hat for Rhinoceros* by Anita Hewett; Brockhampton Press for 'Marmaduke is in a Jam' from *Marmaduke and the Lambs* by Elizabeth Chapman, and 'Two Green Caterpillars' from *Seven Days with Jan* by Mary Cockett; Chatto & Windus Ltd and Richard Hughes for 'The Elephant's Picnic' from *Don't Blame Me*; Helen Clare for 'The Boy Who Ran Away' from *Bel the Giant*; Vera Colwell for 'Tiffy the Squirrel' and 'Pyp Goes to the Country'; Evans Brothers Ltd for 'Johnnikin and the Fox's Tail' from *Here and There Stories* by Rhoda Power; Faber & Faber Ltd and Alison Uttley for 'Tim Rabbit's Bad Day' from *Ten Tales of Tim Rabbit*; Eleanor Farjeon for 'The Green Kitten' from *Jim at the Corner* and 'Cheep!' from *Children's Bells*, both published by the Oxford University Press; Margaret Gore for 'Midsummer Night' and 'The Easter Lamb'; Hamish Hamilton for 'Mustard and Cress' from *The Boy with the Green Thumb* by Barbara Euphan Todd; George G. Harrap & Co. Ltd for 'Susan Smutt' from *The Dawn Shops* by Joyce Lankester Brisley, 'Mary-Mary Earns Some Money' from *Mary-Mary* by Joan G. Robinson, 'The Good Little Christmas Tree' by Ursula Moray Williams, and 'The Little Rooster and the Diamond Button' from *The Good Master* by Kate Seredy (copyright 1935 by Kate Seredy, by permission of Viking Press); John Hopkins for 'The Bus Who Had No Upstairs'; Hutchinson & Co. Ltd for 'Mrs Pepperpot and the Moose' from *Mrs Pepperpot Again* by Alf Prøysen; Methuen & Co. Ltd for 'Nicholas Peabody the Cobbler' from *Travellers' Joy* and 'Farmer Comfort Buys a Pig'

ACKNOWLEDGEMENTS

from *Sugar and Spice* by Ursula Hourihane, 'Noise by Pooh' from *The House at Pooh Corner* by A. A. Milne (Copyright 1928 by E. P. Dutton & Co. Inc., renewal 1956 by A. A. Milne. Reprinted by permission of publisher), 'Ducks' Ditty' reprinted with the permission of Charles Scribner's Sons from *The Wind in the Willows* by Kenneth Grahame, and 'The Train to Glasgow' from *Clinkerdump* by Wilma Horsbrough; Thomas Nelson & Sons Ltd and Richard Wilson for 'The Laughing Dragon' from *The Ever-Ever Land*; Una Norris for 'David's First Flight'; Oliver & Boyd Ltd for 'The Acrobat in the Lilac Tree' from *Our Outdoor Friends* by Irene Byers; Oxford University Press with Leila Berg for 'The Skylark' from *The Nightingale and Other Stories*, with Ian Serraillier for 'The Mouse in the Wainscot' from *The Tale of the Monster Horse*; reprinted by permission of *Punch*, 'The Donkey' by Gertrude Hinde; Ruth D'Arcy Thompson for 'Tumbling Doggie' from *Nursery Nonsense* by D'Arcy W. Thompson; University of London Press for 'Crosspatch' from *Tell Them Again Tales* by Margaret Baker, and 'The Donkey That Helped Father Christmas' from *Twilight and Fireside* and 'The Little Hare and the Tiger' from *More Stories and How to Tell Them*, both by Elizabeth Clark.

Ducks' Ditty

All along the backwater,
Through the rushes tall,
Ducks are a-dabbling,
   Up tails all !

Ducks' tails, drakes' tails,
Yellow feet a-quiver,
Yellow bills all out of sight
   Busy in the river !

Slushy green undergrowth
Where the roach swim –
Here we keep our larder
   Cool and full and dim !

Every one for what he likes !
We like to be
Heads down, tails up,
   Dabbling free !

High in the blue above
Swifts whirl and call –
We are down a-dabbling
  Up tails all !

KENNETH GRAHAME From *The Wind in the Willows*

Tim Rabbit's Bad Day

BY ALISON UTTLEY

Tim Rabbit awoke one morning, late for breakfast. He scrambled out of bed in a hurry, dressed, and ran downstairs. The tea was cold, the toast was flabby, the mushrooms were all eaten! Tim sulked and grumbled, and Mrs Rabbit shook her head at him.

'You got out of bed on the wrong side this morning, Tim,' said she. 'That is why you are so cross.'

That settled it! Tim made up his mind to be naughty all day, and to get some fun out of it, too.

It was a lovely spring day, and the sun shone in the meadow – on the beads of dew, like pearls strung along the grass-blades, and on the cobwebs in the hedge. Tim strolled slowly up the path to school, picking a flower here, cutting a stick there, calling to the echo, stamping on the ground, watching the ants and beetles, dawdling as only a little rabbit can, who doesn't care what happens.

He was so slow that even the snails pricked up their horns, shouldered their houses, and tried to race him. One snail actually got to the old beech-tree where the schoolroom was before Tim arrived, and its brother, too, would have been second if a hungry thrush had not seen it and spoilt the race.

The jays and the magpies mocked him as he wandered along, and little Jenny Wren cried, 'Hurry up, Tim Rabbit. You'll be late and get the stick.'

Tim didn't care, and late he was.

Seven little rabbits sat demurely under the beech-tree, on a

form made of the spreading root. Old Jonathan Rabbit had begun his lesson when Tim sauntered up, with a flower in his button-hole and a dandelion between his lips, for a pipe.

'Puff! Puff! Puff!' went Tim, blowing out rings of imaginary smoke.

'Late again!' said Old Jonathan severely, and the seven little rabbits looked up from their sums, and then nudged one an-

other. 'Look at Tim Rabbit!' said they, whispering behind their paws. 'Isn't he a caution!'

'Come to me!' thundered Old Jonathan, 'and take that dandelion out of your mouth.' He gave Tim a cuff on the head, so that he rolled over on the grass, but of course Tim wasn't hurt, for a rabbit's paws are soft as velvet.

He joined the others on the bench, and repeated his tables after the master. It was Arithmetic and every rabbit picked the green grasses and multiplied by three and by four. When Tim was asked for his answer, he could only shake his head, for he had eaten all the sums!

'Go to the bottom of the class,' cried Old Jonathan crossly, and Tim sat at the end of the row, slyly pushing and poking the next rabbit. 'Pass it on,' he whispered, giving little Jack Rabbit a pinch, and Jack obediently passed it on, so that pinches and nips moved along the row, and soon all the class was wriggling and giggling.

Jonathan looked at them, but did not notice the culprit. It was time for the next lesson, and the rabbits stood in a row ready to begin.

The old rabbit spread a carpet of tiny sticks on the ground, and each little rabbit had to walk across without crackling a twig. Soft paws were daintily raised, as the rabbits leapt and sprang between the network without making a sound. This was the lesson Tim loved, for his feet were small and sensitive, and he could trip through silently. Today, however, just because he was naughty, he danced along so nimbly, on the tips of his toes, with his head in the air, and his ears cocked, that he fell on his nose with a clatter.

Snap! Snap! went the sticks as he rolled among them.

> 'Little Tim Rabbit,
> Up to his tricks,
> Fell on his nose,
> In Jonathan's sticks,'

he chanted as he lay on the ground.

'Jonathan will give you "sticks", Tim Rabbit, if you are not careful,' growled Old Jonathan. 'Go to the bottom of the class.' So again Tim sat meekly at the very end of the bench, whilst the seven little rabbits whispered and chuckled, shaking their heads and peeping admiringly at Tim.

'Isn't Tim naughty today? He must have got out of the wrong side of his bed,' said they.

'Yes,' agreed Tim. 'I climbed out on the side next to the wall. It was difficult, but it's worth it!'

The next lesson was Weather Lesson. Each rabbit had to look at the sky, to feel the wind, to taste the air, and then to say what the day would bring forth – sunshine, or showers, fine or dull.

Old Jonathan stood ready, and the rabbits, one by one, ran out from the shelter of the great tree and gazed at the sky. Now this was a difficult lesson, and they had to use all their wits. They noticed the direction of the wind, and the strength of it as it ruffled their fur. They sniffed the sweet air, smelling for rain or sun. They listened to the birds, whose cries changed with the changing wind.

'Well?' asked Old Jonathan, when they returned to the beech-tree. 'Well? Is it sunshine or shower, storm or fine weather?'

'A sunny day, with hours for play,' answered the seven rabbits, but Tim stayed behind, gazing up in the air with an innocent expression.

'What do you say, Tim?' asked the old rabbit.

> 'Lightning and thunder,
> Snow and hail,
> Rain from a bucket,
> Fog from a pail,'

shouted Tim, turning a somersault.

'Can't you smell the sunshine? Can't you see the clear blue sky? Can't you feel the soft wind from the South?' roared Old Jonathan. 'Go to the bottom of the class.'

But Tim could go no farther, so he sat on the ground.

It was now time for the Smelling Lesson. Jonathan gave each rabbit a dock leaf to bind his eyes, and then the smelling test began.

'What's this?' asked Jonathan, holding up a sprig of wild thyme to the rabbits in turn. Ears twitched, noses wrinkled, paws were held up, as each little animal tried to answer first.

'Please sir, it's wild thyme,' they cried, for they knew the difference between the delicate scent and that of garden thyme.

'What do you say, Tim?' asked Jonathan, for Tim hadn't spoken.

'It's Bed-time,' answered Tim, snoring and rolling over with his eyes shut. But when Tim called a leaf of mint 'Duck and green peas', outraged Jonathan gave Tim such a cuff he fell into a gorse-bush and had to spend the rest of the morning pulling out the prickles.

When lessons were over Tim ran helter-skelter, hoppity-skippity, bumpetty-jump, home again. He leapt over the snails, who were waiting for him down the lane, and knocked their houses off their backs. He whistled to the jay and magpie, mocking their cries. He turned head over heels on an ant

hill, and danced with a hare who came out of the turnip field.

Then he raced to his mother, who was busy getting the dinner ready.

'Mother! Mother!' he cried. 'I've been very naughty today! I *have* enjoyed it. It's been the best day of all the year.'

Alas! Old Jonathan came hobbling to see Mrs Rabbit before the sun set that night. He had a long talk with her and Mr Rabbit about somebody. Little Tim Rabbit stood in a corner of the field, with his nose close to the stone wall, his head bent low, his ears drooping. There he stood in disgrace, and the black and white magpie sat on the wall above him.

'What's the matter, Tim?' it mocked. 'Are you looking for something? What have you lost? Have you mislaid your manners?'

19

'Wait till I'm good,' muttered Tim angrily, 'and then I'll let you see where my manners are!'

The magpie didn't wait, however, for Mrs Rabbit came up.

'Are you good, Tim? Do you feel different?' she asked, anxiously.

Tim sighed. 'Yes. I'm quite good now,' said he. 'A good little feeling has just come to me. May I come out of the corner now?'

'Whatever made you so naughty, Tim?' asked Mrs Rabbit, reprovingly. 'I've never known you to be like this!'

'I got out of bed on the wrong side,' answered Tim. 'I shall jump right out of the middle tomorrow' – and he did.

From *Ten Tales of Tim Rabbit*

Susan Smutt, Who Slept in the Coal-cellar

BY JOYCE LANKESTER BRISLEY

Once upon a time there was a little girl named Susan Smutt.

She had a father and a mother and fifteen brothers and sisters, so you see they needed a fairly big house to live in. But even so it wasn't very easy to find room enough for them all.

Mr and Mrs Smutt slept in the front bedroom; and Annie and Fannie and Pollie and Dollie Smutt slept in the back bedroom; and Willie and Billie and Dickie and Mickie Smutt slept in the top front bedroom; and Tillie and Lillie and Sammie and Hammie Smutt slept in the top back bedroom; and the twins, Cora and Dora Smutt, slept in the attic; and little Angelina Smutt had a bed made up in the bath, as there wasn't another bedroom in the house.

So when Susan Smutt began to get too big to sleep in the bottom drawer in her mother's and father's room any longer the family wondered very much where they could put her.

They looked all over the house, from top to bottom; but there wasn't any room, not even in a cupboard.

And then, just as they were passing the little door leading into the coal-cellar, Susan Smutt called out in her shrill little voice, 'Ooh! Wouldn't it be nice to have a little bedroom in the coal-cellar!'

So, as they couldn't think where else to put her, Mr and Mrs Smutt and all the little Smutts carried the coal in a big box into the scullery; and then they cleaned out the coal-cellar with brooms, and mops, and pails of water; and then they put in a little bed (made out of wooden boxes), and a little chest of

drawers (made out of wooden boxes), and a little chair (made out of wooden boxes), and a little round, red, rag rug.

And every night after that, as soon as the clock struck seven, Susan Smutt said good-night to her father and mother and fifteen brothers and sisters, took up her little night-light, and skipped downstairs to the coal-cellar, to bed!

Susan Smutt thought her little bedroom was the greatest fun in the world!

There was a little round hole in the ceiling, with an iron lid over it, where the men who go round shouting 'Coooooal!' would pour a sackful down into the coal-cellar, if asked (but they weren't). The lid was right in the middle of the pavement (where you must often have seen it in your outings); and when Susan Smutt was in bed she could hear people walking over it, never thinking that they were walking on little Susan Smutt's bedroom window shutter!

Sometimes Susan Smutt would put her little chair on the bed and stand on it, and push up the lid very cautiously and peep out; and if no one was about she could (being very small) pop right out and skip up and down on the pavement in the moonlight, till she heard someone's footsteps come *tramp-tramping* along; then she would pop back to bed and shut the lid before they saw her! In the mornings she could either walk out through her little door to join the family at breakfast or she could climb up through the coal-hole and be taken in at the front door with the milk.

It was great fun.

One morning Susan Smutt was up and out very early, or perhaps the rest of the family was down late; anyhow she had to wait about on the doorstep to be let in.

Presently there came along the road a coal cart, with a big horse walking *clip-clop, clip-clop,* and a big coalman calling, 'Coooooal! Any cooooool?'

When it came opposite the next-door house the next-door door opened, and the next-door lady popped her head out and

said, 'Just put a ton of coal through the coal-hole tomorrow morning, will you?'

And the coalman said, 'Yes, ma'am. Tomorrow morning, ma'am.'

And the next-door lady nodded pleasantly to Susan Smutt, and popped her head in again and shut the next-door door.

When Mrs Smutt opened their door to take in the milk Susan Smutt walked in, saying, 'Good morning, Mother. I'm going to watch the coalman drop a ton of coal through the next-door coal-hole tomorrow morning. Won't that be fun?'

The very next morning Susan Smutt woke up to hear a *clip-clop, clip-clop,* coming along the road. 'Oh,' she said to herself, 'here's the coalman coming. I must hurry.' And she hopped out of bed and pulled on her red woollen stockings.

The coalman shouted, 'Whoooa!' and the coal cart stopped outside. Susan Smutt hurried into her clothes as fast as she could, because she did want to see the coal poured into the next-door coal-hole.

And then – suddenly – what *do* you think? The coalman took the lid off her coal-hole, and started pouring a sackful of coal down on to her little chest of drawers and chair – *bang, bang, rattle!*

'Stop!' cried Susan Smutt, in her shrill little voice. 'This is the wrong coal-hole!'

But the coalman was making such a noise he couldn't hear her. And he poured another sackful of coal down on to her little bed and round, red, rag-rug – *rattle, rattle, crash!*

'Stop! Stop!' cried Susan Smutt.

But the coalman only began to pour another sackful of coal down through the coal-hole – *crash, crash, clatter!*

So Susan Smutt snatched up her red woollen frock from under a heap of coals and fled out of her little door, along the passage, and up the stairs, shouting, 'Father! Mother!' at the top of her voice, all the way.

Well, Father and Mother and fifteen brothers and sisters all came running out of their rooms as if they thought the house was afire. And when they heard what was the matter they all went outside and were very cross with the coalman for making such a mistake. And the next-door lady came out and was very cross with the coalman too. And the poor coalman said he was very sorry, he was sure, but the coal-holes were so close together he quite thought he had got the right one.

Then Mr and Mrs Smutt said, well, as they'd got the coal they'd better keep it now, as it would make such a mess to take it all out again. And the next-door lady said to the coalman, 'Well, just bring me another ton tomorrow.'

And little Susan Smutt wept a little tear down each smutty little cheek, because she hadn't got a bedroom to sleep in.

Then the next-door lady said very kindly, 'Don't cry, Susan Smutt; I've got a nice little bedroom in the attic which I never use. You can have that, and your father shall make a little door through the wall into your house, so that you can reach it from your side !'

So now little Susan Smutt has a nice, sunny little attic bedroom all to herself, just next door to the twins, Cora and Dora Smutt's, room. And every morning she gets up early, and before she has breakfast in her own house she creeps downstairs in the next-door house, and sweeps the kitchen, and makes the fire, and gets the breakfast ready for the next-door lady, just to show how *very* grateful she is for her nice, new little attic bedroom !

From *The Dawn Shops*

The Stamping Elephant

BY ANITA HEWETT

Elephant stamped about in the jungle, thumping down his great grey feet on the grass and the flowers and the small soft animals.

He squashed the tiny shiny creatures and trod on the tails of the creeping creatures. He beat down the corn seedlings, crushed the lilacs, and stamped on the morning glory flowers.

'We must stop all this stamping,' said Goat, Snake, and Mouse.

Goat said, 'Yes, we must stop it. But *you* can't do anything, Mouse.'

And Snake said, 'Of course she can't. Oh no, *you* can't do anything, Mouse.'

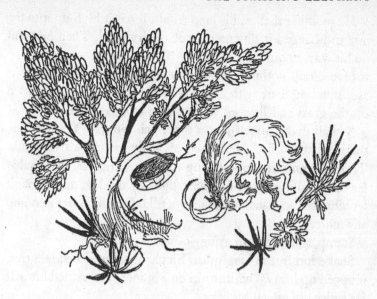

Mouse said nothing. She sat on the grass and listened while Goat told his plan.

'Scare him, that's what I'll do,' said Goat. 'Oh good, good, good, I'll scare old Elephant, frighten him out of his wits, I will.'

He found an empty turtle shell and hung it up on a low branch. Then he beat on the shell with his horns.

'This is my elephant-scaring drum. I shall beat it, clatter, clatter,' he said. 'Elephant will run away. Oh, good, good, good.'

Stamp, stamp, stamp. Along came Elephant.

Goat tossed his head and ran at the shell, clatter, clatter, beating it with his horns.

'Oh, what a clatter I'm making,' he bleated. 'Oh, what a terrible, elephant-scaring, horrible clatter.'

Elephant said '*What* a nasty little noise!'

He took the shell in his long trunk, lifted it high up into the air, and banged it down on Goat's hairy head. Then he went on his way, stamping.

Mouse said nothing. But she thought, 'Poor old Goat looks sad, standing there with a shell on his head.' Then she sat down on the grass and listened while Snake told his plan.

'I shall make myself into a rope,' said Snake. 'Yes, yes, yes, that's what I'll do.' He looped his body around a tree trunk. 'Now I'm an elephant-catching rope. Yes, yes, yes, that's what I am. I shall hold old Elephant tight by the leg, and I shan't let him go. No, I shan't let him go, till he promises not to stamp any more.'

Stamp, stamp, stamp. Along came Elephant.

Snake hid in the long grass. Elephant stopped beside a tree, propped up his two white tusks on a branch, and settled himself for a nice little sleep.

Snake came gliding out of the grass. He looped his long body around the tree trunk and around old Elephant's leg as well. His teeth met his tail at the end of the loop, and he bit on his tail tip, holding fast.

'I have looped old Elephant's leg to the tree trunk. Now I must hold on tight,' he thought.

Elephant woke, and tried to move. But with only three legs he was helpless.

'Why are you holding my leg?' he shouted.

Snake kept quiet. He could not speak. If he opened his mouth the loop would break.

Elephant put his trunk to the ground and filled it with tickling, yellow dust. Then he snorted, and blew the dust at Snake.

Snake wriggled. He wanted to sneeze.

Elephant put his trunk to the ground and sniffed up more of the tickling dust. 'Poof!' he said, and he blew it at Snake.

Snake held his breath and wriggled and squirmed, trying his hardest not to sneeze. But the dust was too tickly. 'Ah ah ah!' He closed his eyes and opened his mouth. 'Ah ah tishoo!' The loop was broken.

Elephant said, '*What* a nasty little cold!'

And he went on his way, stamping.

Mouse said nothing. But she thought, 'Snake looks sad, lying there sneezing his head off.' Then she sat on the grass and made her own plan.

Stamp, stamp, stamp. Along came Elephant. Mouse peeped out of her hole and watched him. He lay on his side, stretched out his legs, and settled himself for a nice long sleep.

Mouse breathed deeply, and stiffened her whiskers. She waited till Elephant closed his eyes. Then she crept through the grass like a little grey shadow, her bright brown eyes watching Elephant's trunk. She made her way slowly around his great feet, and tiptoed past his shining tusks. She trotted along by his leathery trunk until she was close to its tender pink tip. Then suddenly, skip! she darted backwards, and sat in the end of Elephant's trunk.

Elephant opened his eyes, and said: 'Can't I have *any* peace in this jungle? First it's a silly clattering goat, then it's a sillier sneezing snake, and now it's a mouse, the smallest of them all, and quite the silliest. That's what *I* think.'

He looked down his long grey trunk and said, 'Oh yes, I know you are there, little mouse, because I can see your nose and whiskers. Out you get! Do you hear, little mouse?'

'Eek,' said Mouse, 'I won't get out, unless you promise not to stamp.'

'Then I'll shake you out,' Elephant shouted, and he swung his trunk from side to side.

'Thank you,' squeaked Mouse, 'I'm having a ride. It's almost like flying. Thank you, Elephant.'

Elephant shouted, 'I'll drown you out.' He stamped to the river and waded in, dipping the end of his trunk in the water.

'Thank you,' squeaked Mouse, 'I'm having a swim. It's almost like diving. Thank you, Elephant.'

Elephant stood on the bank, thinking. He could not pull down the leaves for his dinner. He could not give himself a bath. He could not live, with a mouse in his trunk.

'Please, little mouse, get out of my trunk. Please,' he said.

'Will you promise not to stamp?' asked Mouse.

'No,' said Elephant.

'Then this is what I shall do,' said Mouse, and she tickled his trunk with her tail.

'Now will you promise not to stamp?'

'No,' said Elephant.

'Then this is what I shall do,' said Mouse and she nipped his trunk with her sharp little teeth.

'Yes,' squealed Elephant. 'Yes, yes, yes.'

Mouse ran back to her hole and waited.

Step, step, step. Along came Elephant, walking gently on great grey feet. He saw the tiny shiny creatures, and waited until they scuttled away. He saw the little creeping creatures, and stepped very carefully over their tails.

'Elephant doesn't stamp any more. *Someone* has stopped him,' the creatures said. 'Someone big and brave and clever.'

Goat said: 'I think Mouse did it.'

And Snake said: 'Oh yes, that is right. Mouse did it.'

And not far away, at the foot of a tree, a small, contented, tired little mouse sat on the grass and smiled to herself.

From *A Hat for Rhinoceros*

The Green Kitten

BY ELEANOR FARJEON

(Jim, an old sailor, tells this story to his friend, Derry, a boy of eight.)

It happened when I was a boy. I felt the call of the sea, and ran away from the farm in Kent where I was born. Our farm was not far from the coast, and soon I came to Pegwell Bay, where the good ship *Rocking-horse* was riding at anchor.

The Captain saw me coming, through his telescope, and when I was near enough he called, 'Come here, boy!' He had a commanding sort of voice, so I came.

He looked me up and down, and said, 'My cabin-boy has just run away to go on a farm.'

'That's funny,' I said, 'because I've just run away from a farm to go for a cabin-boy.'

The Captain looked me up and down, and said, 'You'll do. What's your name?'

'Jim,' I said. 'What's yours?'

'Cap'n Potts,' he said. 'Well, Jim, we don't sail till tomorrow, and tonight I feel like shrimps.'

'Like shrimps?' I said.

'Yes, like shrimps,' said Cap'n Potts.

Now when he said he was feeling like shrimps, I thought Cap'n Potts meant he was feeling sad, or seedy, or something like that. But it turned out he meant just what he said, for he handed me a big shrimping-net, and said, 'Go and catch some.'

That was a job any boy would enjoy, be he cabin-boy or farm-boy. I kicked off my boots in a jiffy, and went shrimping among the pools on the beach. The pools were surrounded by

rocks, and the rocks were covered with thick green weed, like wet hair, very slippery to the feet.

When I'd got a nice netful of shrimps, I took them aboard the *Rocking-horse* and Cap'n Potts said, 'Well done, Jim! You'll make a first-class cabin-boy, I see. Take them below to Cookie, and tell him to boil them for tea.'

I went below and found Cookie, and said, 'Please, I'm Jim the new cabin-boy, please, and please Cap'n Potts says will you please cook these shrimps for tea?'

'Shrimps!' said Cookie. 'Do you call *this* a shrimp?'

He plunged his hand into the net, and fetched up what looked like a little lump of rock smothered in green seaweed. But the little lump wriggled in Cookie's hand, the little lump arched its weedy green back, the little lump waved a weedy green tail, the little lump pricked up two weedy green ears, the little lump wrinkled its weedy green nose, and *spat*. Next thing, it jumped out of Cookie's big hands, and clawed its way up to my shoulder, where it sat rubbing its soft green head against my cheek.

The little lump was nothing less than a wee green Kitten, with eyes as pink as coral.

The next day, when *we* sailed, the Kitten sailed too, and before long it was the pet of the ship. But I was its favourite, and it always slept in my cabin. Being the cabin-boy, I had, of course, a cabin to myself.

Now that first trip of mine we did not seem to have the best of luck. Everything the ship could have the *Rocking-horse* had, like a child who has chicken-pox, measles, and mumps, one after the other. The *Rocking-horse* had hurricanes, and icebergs, and pirates, and thunderbolts. Once she was wrecked, and once she was becalmed.

It was when she was becalmed that *my* adventure happened.

Cap'n Potts was a restless man, and liked to be on the move. It gave him the fidgets when the ship got stuck like that in the middle of the sea, and one evening he came up to me and said, 'Jim, I feel like lobsters!'

'Never mind, Cap'n,' I said. 'Perhaps we'll get a move on tomorrow.'

'Perhaps we will,' said Cap'n Potts, 'and perhaps we won't. But whether we do or don't, tonight I feel like lobsters.' Then he handed me a lobster-pot, and said, 'Go and catch some.'

Then I saw what he meant, and I got into a diving-suit, tucked the lobster-pot under my arm, dived over the side of the *Rocking-horse*, and sank to the bottom.

There was I, just a little nipper, all alone on the bed of the ocean. And there I saw wonders, to be sure! Coral and pearl and golden sands, coloured sea-weed as big as bushes, sunfish and moonfish like red-and-silver jewels, anemones like brilliant beds of flowers, and a sunken ship painted with gold and vermilion, like the castle of a king. The only thing I didn't see was lobsters.

I was just wondering how to catch what wasn't there, when I found I was caught myself. The long arm of an Octopus had shot out and whipped round me like a rope; next thing I knew, I was lifted up and dropped down into the state-room of the gorgeous ship I mentioned.

There I found myself face to face with an angry Catfish. She was the biggest Catfish you ever saw, and on her head was a little coral crown. She kept opening and shutting her mouth at me, and goggling her eyes at me, as cross as two sticks, and I couldn't think why.

'You seem upset, ma'am,' I said.

'Upset!' she snapped. 'I should think I am upset! And on top of it all you must go and call me ma'am, as though I hadn't a royal title of my own.'

'Tell me what it is, and I'll call you by it, ma'am,' said I.

'There you go again!' she snapped. 'Where are your eyes,

boy? Can't you see the crown on my head? I am the Queen of the Catfish, and I want my Kitten!'

'Your Kitten, ma'am-your-majesty?' said I.

'My Kitten, booby,' said she, 'that you caught in your shrimping-net. And till Cap'n Potts gives it me back, he shan't have his cabin-boy. As long as he keeps my Kitten, I'll keep *you*!'

'Who's to let him know?' I asked.

'You shall write him a letter,' said she, 'and I'll send it up by Octopus.'

With that she set me down in the ship's saloon, a very glorious room indeed, with golden plate and jewelled goblets on the tables, and hangings of rich leather on the walls. I took off my diving-suit, pulled out my notebook and pencil, and scribbled a note to Cap'n Potts. This was it:

Dear Cap'n Potts,

The Queen of the Catfish wants her Kittenfish, which is the green Kitten we've got aboard the Rocking-horse, *and she's going to keep me till she gets it, so if you want me back send down the Kitten by Octopus, but if you'd rather have the Kitten than me, don't bother. I hope you are well, as this leaves me.*

Yours obediently,

Jim

Just as I scribbled 'Jim', the Queen of the Catfish looked up and said, 'Is your letter done? The Octopus is ready to start.'

'Here's the letter, ma'am-your-majesty,' said I, 'but I'm afraid the pencil won't stand salt water.'

'We'll put it in a shell to keep it dry,' said the Queen of the Catfish. The saloon was littered with junk of all sorts, and she picked out a big spotted shell with a mouth like a letter-box. Then she posted my letter in the shell, gave it to the Octopus, and he went aloft.

I wondered a bit whether Cap'n Potts would rather keep the Kitten than have me back again. I would in his place, and I made ready to stay under the sea for the rest of my life. It wasn't a bad place to stay in, but I preferred the *Rocking-horse*. So when the Octopus came down again with the Kitten in its tentacle, I felt quite light-hearted.

It was a pretty sight to see that little green Kitten leap into its mother's fins, sea-mewing with pleasure; and the Queen of the Catfish was so pleased to see it that she turned from snarly to smiley.

'Get into your diving-suit, Jim,' she said, 'and my respects to your Captain, and tell him the next time he catches a Kittenfish he must throw it back, or there'll be trouble.'

'There *was* trouble,' said I, 'what with hurricanes, icebergs, pirates, and all.'

'Those were my doing,' said the Queen of the Catfish, 'but from now on you shall have fair winds and smooth sailing. Here's your lobster-pot.' With that she handed me my pot, and it was full to the brim with lobsters. 'Nasty vicious things!' said she. 'Always nipping my kittens when they get the chance. I'm glad to be rid of a few. Good-bye, Jim.'

'Good-bye, ma'am-your-majesty,' said I.

'Booby!' said she.

The Octopus took me in one tentacle, and the lobster-pot in another; the Kitten waved its paw at me, and the Queen of the Catfish kissed her fin, and up we went. In another moment I and the lobsters were put down safe and sound on the deck of the good ship *Rocking-horse*, and wasn't I glad! I'd never thought to see her more.

Cap'n Potts was sorry to lose the Kitten, but when he saw the lobsters he said, 'Well done, my lad; you're an A-One Cabin-boy, you are!' Then the wind began to blow, and the sails began to fill, and the *Rocking-horse* was well under way when we all sat down to hot lobsters for tea.

From *Jim at the Corner*

The Boy Who Ran Away

BY HELEN CLARE

There was once a little boy who was walking in the park, kicking at his toes and looking for adventures. He did not like his mother holding his hand, and he did not like his sister because everybody noticed her as she sat in her pram and waved her rattle.

Now they had not gone very far when they came to the pond with ducks floating on it, and everybody watching them. The little boy's mother also stopped to watch them, and then by chance let go of his hand.

'Aha!' thought the little boy, 'now I'll run away.'

So he took to his heels and he ran and he ran. He had not

gone very far before he met a scooter, a bright yellow scooter, scooting up the paths on its bright red wheels.

'Hey!' said the little boy. 'Where are you going?'

'I'm going for a scoot. Would you like to come with me?'

'Yes,' said the little boy, and off they scooted.

They hadn't gone far before they met a tricycle, a bright blue tricycle pedalling up the pathway.

'Hey!' said the little boy, 'where are you going? I ran away from mummy until I met this scooter.'

'Oh,' said the tricycle, 'I'm going to meet a friend of mine. Want to come with me?'

'Yes,' said the little boy, and off they pedalled. They hadn't gone far before they met a bicycle, a black and silver bicycle, ringing its bell.

'Hey!' said the little boy, 'where are you going? I ran away from mummy until I met a scooter. And I scooted on the scooter until I met a tricycle.'

'I see,' said the bicycle, putting both its brakes on. 'I'm going for a fast spin. Like to come with me?'

'Yes,' said the little boy. So off they bicycled.

They pedalled and they pedalled to the top of a steep hill, and flew down at a great rate not pedalling at all.

'Phew!' said the little boy, 'that was lovely!'

They hadn't gone far when they met a new motor-car, a brand new motor-car, hooting on its hooter.

'Hey!' said the little boy, 'where are you off to? I ran away from mummy until I met a scooter, and I scooted on the scooter until I met a tricycle, and I pedalled on the tricycle until I met this bicycle.'

'Ha, ha!' said the motor-car, 'I'm going for a joy-ride. Care to come with me, on my new leather cushions?'

'Yes,' said the little boy, climbing in eagerly. So off they went, with the road spinning under them.

They hadn't gone far, when they overtook an omnibus, a great red omnibus with a great gloomy face.

'If you want to go farther, just whistle to that omnibus, because this is where I live,' said the brand new motor-car.

'Hey!' said the little boy, 'where are you heading for? I ran away from mummy until I met a scooter, and I scooted on the scooter until I met a tricycle, and I pedalled on the tricycle until I met a bicycle, and I cycled on the bicycle until I met that motor-car.'

'Humph!' said the omnibus, 'I'm going to the country. If you want to come with me, you'd better get aboard.'

'All right,' said the little boy, jumping on the omnibus, and off went the omnibus climbing up a hill.

It groaned and it grumbled and then it started humming, and then it sang right up the scale and had to start again.

Now, they'd gone a good distance when they saw a green engine puffing and panting along a railway bridge.

'This is where I stop,' said the bus to the little boy. 'You'd better catch that train if you're going on again.'

'Hi!' said the little boy, 'where are you making for? I ran away from mummy until I met a scooter and I scooted on the scooter until I met a tricycle, and I pedalled on the tricycle until I met a bicycle, and I cycled on the bicycle until I met a motor-car and I whizzed off in the motor-car until I met this omnibus.'

'Pouff!' said the green train, taking its top hat off, 'I'm going to the sea-side, much faster than a bus. Jump in if you want to, I haven't time to dally.'

'Rather,' said the little boy, and scrambled up the engine, and off went the haughty train: 'Pouff! pouff! pouff!'

They panted through the countryside with smoke curling round them, until at last the little boy spied the great sea.

'I don't cross the channel, though I could if I wanted to! Pouff!' said the green train, 'I don't like the sea. If you want to go over, you'd better hail a steamer. They're rather large and vulgar things, if you ask me. And not content with one top hat, they flourish two or three.'

'Ahoy!' said the little boy, waving to a steamer, 'where are you sailing to, I'd like to know? I ran away from mummy until I met a scooter and I scooted on the scooter until I met a tricycle and I pedalled on the tricycle until I met a bicycle, and I cycled on the bicycle until I met a motor-car, and I whizzed off in the motor-car until I met an omnibus, and I jolted in the omnibus until I met an engine.'

'Hoots!' said the steamer, 'I'm sailing to the Continent. If you want to come too, I'll let down the gangway.'

'I do,' said the little boy, and ran aboard the ship.

'Hoo-oots!' said the steamer dipping through the water, and it wasn't very long before they reached the other side.

Now just as they were docking they saw a silver aeroplane.

'There,' boomed the steamer, 'you'd better catch that.'

'Hullo-o!' cried the little boy, putting both his hands up. 'Where are you flying to next, if you please? I ran away from mummy until I met a scooter and I scooted on the scooter until I met a tricycle, I pedalled on the tricycle until I met a bicycle, and I cycled on the bicycle until I met a motor-car. I whizzed off in the motor-car until I met an omnibus, I jolted in the omnibus until I met an engine, and I panted in the engine until I met a steamer.'

'M-m-m-m-m,' said the aeroplane. 'I'm going back to England. Want to come with me?'

'Yes, please,' said the little boy, and clambered up the steps.

'M-m-m-mind,' said the aeroplane, climbing up the cloud banks. 'Put your head inside, or you'll lose it in the clouds.'

They went so fast they were back in a twinkling and landed at the aerodrome about five o'clock.

On his way home the little boy saw a postman, standing in the street with a sack on his back.

'I say!' said the little boy, 'where are you going? I ran away from mummy until I met a scooter and I scooted on the scooter until I met a tricycle, and I pedalled on the tricycle until I met a bicycle, and I cycled on the bicycle until I met a motor-car. I whizzed off in the motor-car until I met an omnibus, I jolted in the omnibus until I met an engine, and I panted in the engine until I met a steamer, and I sailed off in the steamer until I met an aeroplane.'

'Umph!' said the postman, putting his sack down. 'I am a postman delivering the last post.'

'Oh?' said the little boy. 'Do you go near Croydon?'

'Yes,' said the postman, 'I know where you live. Hop in the sack and I'll give you a ride.'

So they walked till they came to a house in Croydon, with a fence around it and a garden in the front.

'Now,' said the postman, 'I'll knock on the door knocker, and when the door opens, out you jump.'

So the little boy got ready, laughing in his coat sleeve, and the postman knocked: 'Rat-a-tat-tat!'

And when the door opened, the postman said, 'A parcel.' And out jumped the little boy: 'Bo! bo! bo! I ran away from mummy until I met a scooter and I scooted on the scooter until I met a tricycle and I pedalled on the tricycle until I met a bicycle and I cycled on the bicycle until I met a motor-car. I whizzed off in the motor-car until I met an omnibus, and I jolted in the omnibus until I met an engine, I panted in the engine until I met a steamer, and I sailed off in the steamer until I met an aeroplane, I floated in the aeroplane until I met the postman! AND HE'S BROUGHT ME WITH THE LETTERS IN THE VERY LAST POST!'

So they thanked the postman kindly and said, 'Good evening.' And the little boy was very glad to see all his family, and the family were very glad to see the little boy. And as he was so hungry, they gave him lots of supper. He had all the things he liked the best before he went to bed.

From *Bel the Giant and Other Stories*

Just for Fun

Have you heard of the man
   Who stood on his head,
And put his clothes
   Into his bed,
And folded himself
   On a chair instead?

ANON

There was a little Boy, and he had a little Dog;
   And he taught that Dog to beg;
And that dear little Dog all dinner-time,
   Would stand upon one leg.

One day to his master's great surprise,
   That little Dog said, 'Here goes,'
And he cock'd his hind-legs up in the air,
   And stood upon his nose.

D'ARCY W. THOMPSON

One day a boy went walking,
 And walked into a store.
He bought a pound of sausage meat,
 And laid it on the floor.
The boy began to whistle –
 He whistled up a tune,
And all the little sausages
 Danced around the room.

ANON

There was an old man called Michael Finnegan,
He grew whiskers on his chinnegan,
The wind came out and blew them in again –
Poor old Michael Finnegan – Begin again !

ANON

The Elephant's Picnic

BY RICHARD HUGHES

Elephants are generally clever animals, but there was once an elephant who was very silly; and his great friend was a kangaroo. Now, kangaroos are not often clever animals, and this one certainly was not, so she and the elephant got on very well together.

One day they thought they would like to go off for a picnic by themselves. But they did not know anything about picnics, and had not the faintest idea of what to do to get ready.

'What do you do on a picnic?' the elephant asked a child he knew.

'Oh, we collect wood and make a fire, and then we boil the kettle,' said the child.

'What do you boil the kettle for?' said the elephant in surprise.

'Why, for tea, of course,' said the child in a snapping sort of way; so the elephant did not like to ask any more questions. But he went and told the kangaroo, and they collected together all the things they thought they would need.

When they got to the place where they were going to have their picnic, the kangaroo said that she would collect the wood because she had got a pouch to carry it back in. A kangaroo's pouch, of course, is very small; so the kangaroo carefully chose the smallest twigs she could find, and only about five or six of those. In fact, it took a lot of hopping to find any sticks small enough to go in her pouch at all; and it was a long time before she came back. But silly though the elephant was, he soon saw those sticks would not be enough for a fire.

'Now *I* will go off and get some wood,' he said.

His ideas of getting wood were very different. Instead of taking little twigs he pushed down whole trees with his forehead, and staggered back to the picnic-place with them rolled up in his trunk. Then the kangaroo struck a match, and they lit a bonfire made of whole trees. The blaze, of course, was enormous, and the fire was so hot that for a long time they could not get near it; and it was not until it began to die down a bit that they were able to get near enough to cook anything.

'Now, let's boil the kettle,' said the elephant. Amongst the things he had brought was a brightly shining copper kettle and a very large black iron saucepan. The elephant filled the saucepan with water.

'What are you doing that for?' said the kangaroo.

'To boil the kettle in, you silly,' said the elephant. So he popped the kettle in the saucepan of water, and put the saucepan on the fire; for he thought, the old juggins, that you boil a kettle in the same way you boil an egg, or boil a cabbage! And the kangaroo, of course, did not know any better.

So they boiled and boiled the kettle, and every now and then they prodded it with a stick.

'It doesn't seem to be getting tender,' said the elephant sadly, 'and I'm sure we can't eat it for tea until it does.'

So then away he went and got more wood for the fire; and still the saucepan boiled and boiled, and still the kettle remained as hard as ever. It was getting late now, almost dark.

'I am afraid it won't be ready for tea,' said the kangaroo. 'I am afraid we shall have to spend the night here. I wish we had got something with us to sleep in.'

'Haven't you?' said the elephant. 'You mean to say you didn't pack before you came away?'

'No,' said the kangaroo. 'What should I have packed anyway?'

'Why, your trunk, of course,' said the elephant. 'That is what people pack.'

'But I haven't got a trunk,' said the kangaroo.

'Well, I have,' said the elephant, 'and I've packed it! Kindly pass the pepper; I want to unpack!'

So then the kangaroo passed the elephant the pepper, and the elephant took a good sniff. Then he gave a most tremendous sneeze, and everything he had packed in his trunk shot out of

it – tooth-brush, spare socks, gym shoes, a comb, a bag of bull's-eyes, his pyjamas, and his Sunday suit. So then the elephant put on his pyjamas and lay down to sleep; but the kangaroo had no pyjamas, and so, of course, she could not possibly sleep.

'All right,' she said to the elephant; 'you sleep and I will sit up and keep the fire going.'

So all night the kangaroo kept the fire blazing brightly and the kettle boiling merrily in the saucepan. When the next morning came the elephant woke up.

'Now,' he said, 'let's have our breakfast.'

So they took the kettle out of the saucepan; and what do you think? *It was boiled as tender as tender could be!* So they cut it fairly in half and shared it between them, and ate it for breakfast; and both agreed they had never had so good a breakfast in their lives.

From *Don't Blame Me and Other Stories*

Tiffy the Squirrel

BY VERA COLWELL

It was Springtime when Tiffy, the grey squirrel, came running through the woods, followed by another squirrel. They were searching for a suitable tree where they could build a house for themselves.

They ran up the trunk of a tall tree, peeping into the holes to see who lived there, and sprang from one branch to another.

'Ah, this is better,' said Tiffy. He had reached a place almost at the top of the tree where two branches forked. 'We will build it just here,' he said, and they both set to work.

Up and down the tree they ran, collecting twigs and leaves and bits of bark, until they had made their house. It was round like a ball, with a hole in the side, and they called it a drey.

'All we want now,' said Tiffy, 'is some moss to line it with and make it cosy.' They ran down again and searched busily round the roots of the trees and the rocks. Bit by bit they carried scraps of moss up the tree and made a soft lining for their new home.

'How tired I am!' yawned Mrs Tiffy and, after eating a few nuts, they curled up in their drey and fell fast asleep.

Tiffy and his little wife were very happy in the green wood. There was plenty to eat there – fresh shoots and buds on the trees, beech nuts and acorns and pine cones on the ground. Sometimes they even robbed a bird's nest and ate the eggs.

One sunny day such a noise and bustle went on at the top of the tree. 'Chuck! Chuck!' cried Tiffy to another squirrel who had come to see what was the matter. 'Don't come near here!'

He chased the other squirrel away and ran down the trunk looking very important. Once on the ground he curled his tail over his back proudly. He had a secret!

He ate a few shoots and nuts, then climbed up the trunk again to see that all was well.

'Why, look!' shouted an inquisitive blackbird, peering into the mouth of the drey. Inside were four baby squirrels. What funny looking little creatures they were. They were pink and hairless and they couldn't see. Their mother was keeping them snug and warm.

The baby squirrels grew fast. Then their eyes opened and they began to be covered with coats of silky down. Their long tails were soon bushy like their mother's and Tiffy's.

Tiffy took great care that no enemy came near them, but they were so high up in the tree that there was not much danger.

Then came the time when the little squirrels must learn to run about the trees as Tiffy did.

Tiffy called them out on to a branch. 'Use your tails to steady yourselves,' he said, 'and put them flat along the branch when you run. It's quite easy.'

The little squirrels didn't think it was at all easy. They were afraid at first, but before long they were running about the top of the tree. As each squirrel reached the ground, it curled its bushy tail over its back as Tiffy did. Up went all the pointed ears and Tiffy and his wife watched proudly. They were really very handsome squirrels indeed!

Now they had to learn how to find their food. Tiffy led them over the grass and round the trees and they found tasty green shoots and roots and pine cones.

'Come and see what I've found!' chattered Tiffy excitedly. There under the roots of the tree were some nuts hidden away. What a feast they had!

'Don't wander away!' said Tiffy. 'The stoat may be near. He has sharp teeth and he is strong enough to kill you. Look out for him always. The fox is our enemy too, but he doesn't often come this way, thank goodness.'

The little squirrels listened quietly, a nut in their paws and their bushy tails curled over their backs, but they quickly forgot all about stoats and scampered everywhere after each other.

Soon their mother called to them. They ran up the trunk of the tree and the sun shining through the leaves showed up their silvery grey fur and the brown on their necks. Now they were learning to spring from branch to branch, landing with their front paws outstretched.

Their mother had a surprise for them. 'You are so big now,' she said, 'that some of you will have to have a separate house. There is not enough room in our old house for us all. We shall fall out!'

So everyone set to work and made an extra house. It was great fun but how tired they were when it was finished at last.

As Autumn came and the warm sunny days passed, the squirrels hunted for food and, when they had eaten all they could, buried the rest. They knew there would not be much to eat in the wood when the cold days of winter came. Busily they gathered nuts and hid them away under the fallen leaves or under the roots of the trees. But they soon forgot where they had hidden them and were very surprised when they found them again!

Winter came and the cold winds blew. Now the squirrels spent most of their time in their dreys. They curled their tails round and slept warm and cosy. When the sun came out on a warm day, they uncurled themselves and ran down to find some hidden nuts or tender bits of root. Sometimes they even ventured out when there was snow on the ground, leaping over the drifts in search of food.

If they were very hungry, Tiffy would lead them to a place where people lived, for human beings put nuts and food out for birds. At first they were afraid to go near, then, greatly daring, Tiffy or one of his children, darted across the lawn and snatched a nut. Nibble, nibble! and the titbit was gone. Away dashed the squirrel again with a whisk of its tail.

But at last the winter was over. How glad the squirrels were to feel the warm touch of the sunshine and to hear the call of the birds. Once more they scampered along the branches and up and down the tree trunk, leaping for joy in the sunlight.

'Chuck! Chuck!' they cried. 'Here we are again!'

The Donkey That Helped
Father Christmas

BY ELIZABETH CLARK

It was Christmas Eve and the night was very quiet and still. The stars and the little moon sparkled in the sky and the hoarfrost sparkled on the grass. It was a bright clear night, but it was very cold.

The old Donkey who lived on the common was limping along towards a great clump of tall ragged furze-bushes. He knew of a sheltered place in the middle of the clump – almost like a little cave. It would be warmer there, and he might find a tuft of grass, that was not frosted, to eat when morning came.

He was a rough-coated, shaggy old Donkey who had been left behind by some gipsies who had camped on the common in the spring, because he was too lame to pull their little cart. He had lived there ever since. He was still rather lame, but he limped about slowly and comfortably and munched grass and green leaves. He was glad there was no heavy load to pull along hard roads and rough lanes and nobody to beat his poor little back with a thick stick. Nobody was unkind to him. In fact, nobody noticed him; he was just a shaggy, shabby old Donkey.

Sometimes he would have liked a little more company. Donkeys are friendly creatures, and he missed the old white horse that drew the gipsies' van and the little brown dog that barked so loudly and the little black cat that sat on the steps of the van blinking and purring when the sun shone. He even missed the children, though they had teased him and bothered him by climbing on his tired old back to ride.

That Christmas Eve the Donkey was feeling very lonely. The brown cow that lived on the common had been driven into her shed because the weather had turned so cold. She was glad to go, and the Donkey had heard the old woman who came to fetch her say: 'Come along, Brownie; come along, my dear, into your nice warm shed. There's some warm straw and some beautiful hay and a feed of chopped swedes for a treat, because tomorrow is Christmas Day.' (Swedes are like very big turnips and cows like them very much.)

The Donkey had heard of Christmas. He did not know much about it, but if it was anything to do with hay and turnips he was sure it must be comfortable. He had once tasted a turnip-top and now and again he had a mouthful of hay that had been stolen from somebody's stack.

'Hay and chopped swedes,' he said to himself, 'hay and chopped swedes.' The thought made him feel hungry, and he put his nose down and snuffled and blew among the grass tufts and tried to find something to eat. But the grass was all stiff and frosted. It tickled his nose and made him sneeze and sneeze.

'Broo-oo-oof,' said the Donkey (which is as near as I can get to writing down a donkey's sneeze for you). He shook his head hard till his ears flapped, and brayed a long mournful bray.

'Eee-aw-ee-aw-ee-aw-ee-aw-aw-aw-*aw*,' said the Donkey. He ended with a kind of choky snort and stood there with his neck stretched out and his ears laid back and his tail tucked in between his legs – a sad, shaggy, grumpy old Donkey.

Down in the valley where the village stood the church clock began to strike just as he finished braying. It struck twelve; each stroke sounded loud and clear in the stillness. And as it finished striking there came another sound. You and I might never have heard it, it was so tiny and soft. But animals can hear a great many more things than most people – and can see them too. The Donkey pricked up his ears and stood listening.

There was a little shivery, silvery tinkling in the air, a pretty, tiny, far-off sound as if the stars above were tingling. It came nearer and nearer still. Then it seemed to the Donkey that somewhere overhead something went rushing by with a clear, sweet ringing like silver bells and a noise of far-away hoofs galloping fast.

It was an exciting kind of noise. It made the Donkey feel as if he must gallop too. He could not remember galloping since he was a baby donkey with his mother; all his life had been spent jog-trotting with a cart. But he tucked in his head and his ears and his tail as donkeys do when they gallop, and he was just going to try – in spite of his game leg – when he heard another sound. Somebody was coming up the hill.

The Donkey waited and listened. He could hear footsteps crunching a little on the frosty grass. Presently he could see somebody coming towards him – somebody tall and big in a long shaggy white fur coat with a warm white fur hood pulled over his head and big fur-topped boots upon his feet. As he came nearer, the Donkey could see that he had a long white beard and under his white fur hood his eyes shone and twinkled like two bright stars. There was a big sack upon his shoulders. It was tied in the middle, but both ends bulged and hung down as if it was full of queerly shaped things.

He came and stood by the Donkey. He was puffing a little as if the sack was heavy to carry up the hill. His breath was like a little cloud in the frosty air. He looked at the Donkey and the Donkey looked at him.

The Donkey was feeling still more excited; he was happy too, not grumpy any more. There seemed to be a wonderful, kind, warm, friendly feeling all around. He was remembering something the brown cow had told him about Christmas Eve and he was longing to ask a question. But he thought it would be more polite to wait till he was spoken to, so he stayed still and quiet. And then a very kind voice said: 'Happy Christmas, friend Donkey. I heard you calling and you sounded lonely, so I came.'

'I *was* lonely,' said the Donkey, 'and I'm glad you came. Excuse my asking, but would you mind telling me who you are?'

And the friendly voice said: 'Some people call me Father Christmas and some say Santa Klaus. It's all the same really. They both stand for loving-kindness.'

'I remember now,' said the Donkey; 'the brown cow told me about you. But *she* said,' said the Donkey in a puzzled voice, 'that you came in a sledge with reindeer.'

'So I do,' said Father Christmas. 'So I do. But I've sent them home tonight. It's after twelve o'clock. Didn't you hear the sledge-bells go by?'

'Oh-h-h l' said the Donkey, 'so *that* was it.'

'Yes,' said Father Christmas, 'that was it. They've been a long, long way tonight. Here, there, and everywhere we've been, all over the country – north, south, east, and west – finding the children. Children from Birmingham, children from Bristol, children from London, and children from Plymouth, children from Newcastle and Liverpool and Hull and ever so many other places. Out of the towns they've gone and into the country. All over the place they are this Christmas, and wherever they are we've found them.'

'So when twelve o'clock struck,' said Father Christmas, "Home!" I said to the reindeer. I tied up the reins and let

66

them go, and off they went to their stable. There's only this sackful now to take to Green Lane Hollow and a few places on the way. I can carry that myself.'

The Donkey looked at the sack. It was large and it was bulgy and certainly it was heavy.

'Green Lane Hollow is twelve miles away,' he said. He knew all the lanes and hills and hollows. He had pulled his little cart up hill and down dale all round the country with the gipsies.

Father Christmas smiled at him. 'If I keep on walking,' he said, 'I shall get there.'

'Couldn't I help?' said the Donkey. 'I could carry the sack.'

'Why,' said Father Christmas, 'so you could.' He looked at the Donkey very affectionately. 'But what about your leg?'

'I can manage,' said the Donkey stoutly.

'So you shall,' said Father Christmas. 'So you shall.'

He laid the sack across the Donkey's back and they set out. Across the common they went and down a narrow lane; up a steep hill and along the high-road. On and on they went. The sack was heavy, but the Donkey's back was strong, and though his leg was stiff it was wonderful how little it hurt.

On and on they went. Sometimes the road dipped into hollows where it was dark; then Father Christmas went ahead, to show the way. There was a kind of shining round about him and it was quite easy to follow him.

But mostly he walked beside the Donkey with his hand resting on the Donkey's shoulders, just where the dark cross-mark showed on the shaggy mouse-coloured coat. It gave the Donkey a wonderful happy kind of warm glow to feel it there.

Every now and again they stopped to leave a packet or a bundle by the door of a house or cottage. The Donkey could feel that the sack was growing lighter. But there was still a good deal left in it when they came to the top of the long lane that led down to Green Lane Hollow.

Father Christmas looked up at the sky and nodded. 'It's not long now till daylight,' he said.

It certainly was a long lane. The stars were beginning to look pale and silvery and there was a pinky look in the sky before they came to the bottom of the hill and saw a long white cottage with a thatched roof. It looked like a little farm. There were comfortable little noises of hens clucking and waking and a cow lowing in a shed.

The house looked fast asleep. All the windows were dark and all the curtains were drawn. But as the Donkey and Father Christmas came down the road they saw a little chink of light in a window and smoke began to fluff out of a chimney.

'That's old Mrs Honeywell,' said Father Christmas. 'She's

stirring up the fire. The house will be wide awake in a moment. It's time for me to be going.'

They went quietly along, walking on the grass at the edge of the lane. As they came to the door they could hear Mrs Honeywell trotting about, clattering cups and saucers and clacketing to and fro over the brick floor.

'Happy Christmas,' said Father Christmas softly to the Donkey. He stooped and kissed him on his velvety nose. His beard was warm and tickly and soft. The Donkey wanted to sneeze – but the sneeze turned into a bray – a most tremendous bray.

'Ee-aw-ee-aw-ee-aw,' said the Donkey. He heard someone give a little chuckle and he felt something touch his ears. He looked about, but Father Christmas was gone.

But the cottage was awake – wide awake. The door flew open and there stood old Mrs Honeywell. The curtains rustled back and the windows creaked up and there was Master Honeywell leaning out of one window and two small boys at the next window and two more at the window beyond. They were all staring at the Donkey. And who wouldn't stare if they looked out of their window on Christmas Day in the morning and saw a Donkey standing there, with a sack upon his back?

'Bless me!' said Mrs Honeywell. 'Where did *that* come from? Bless me!' she said again, 'it's got a ticket on its head!'

She came close to the Donkey and looked. Father Christmas had left a message. Hanging to the Donkey's ears was a neat little label. It said: 'I bring Happy Christmas to Green Lane Hollow.'

'Well, I never *did*!' said Mrs Honeywell. 'Come along down, Father – come along, Dick and Tommy and Charlie and John.'

The four boys came tumbling downstairs with Master Honeywell behind them. They had had lots of surprises since they

came out of London to live with Master and Mrs Honeywell –
but this was the biggest surprise of all.

Mrs Honeywell patted the Donkey and gave him an apple
to eat. Then she turned the sack out on the kitchen floor.

There was a football and four red jerseys for the boys. There

was a warm blue woollen coat for Mrs Honeywell and a knitted
waistcoat for Master Honeywell. There was a plum-pudding
in a basin and a bottle of sweets. No wonder the sack had felt
bumpy!

But the boys seemed to think the Donkey was the best Christmas present of all. They patted him and petted him. Mrs
Honeywell gave him another apple and Master Honeywell
gave him an armful of hay. Everyone was happy and kind, and
I believe the Donkey was happiest of all.

That was Christmas Day, and he has been there ever since.
He has grown quite sleek; the boys have brushed and curry-
combed his coat. Master Honeywell has doctored his lame leg,
and sometimes he pulls a little cart that is never too heavily

loaded and trots along the road to the village when Mrs Honeywell goes shopping.

He helps with the hay-harvest in the summer, and when the
boys are not in school, one or other of them is generally on his
back. He is a happy and contented old Donkey.

From *Twilight and Fireside*

The Sleeping Beauty

TRADITIONAL

Once upon a time a beautiful little girl was born to a King and Queen. Seven fairies were invited to her christening, but unfortunately the King forgot to ask one old and wicked fairy. She came to the christening but how angry she was that she had been forgotten!

One by one, six of the fairies gave the little Princess the loveliest gifts in the world, but before the seventh could step forward, the wicked fairy hobbled up to the cradle.

'When the Princess is fifteen years old, she shall prick her finger with a spindle and die!' she said with a horrible laugh.

'Alas, alas!' cried everyone and the Queen began to weep. But the King shouted: 'Catch that old woman! We must make her undo her spell.'

But the wicked fairy had disappeared and, search as they might, she could not be found.

The seventh fairy came up to the cradle and, touching the little baby gently, she said: 'I cannot undo all the harm the wicked fairy has done, but my magic is strong enough to help a little. When the Princess pricks her finger, she shall not die but sleep for a hundred years. At the end of that time, a Prince shall awaken her.'

Fifteen years is a long time and everyone hoped that something would happen before then to save the Princess. So the King made a royal command that every spindle in the kingdom should be destroyed. 'If there are no spindles, my daughter cannot prick herself on one!' he said and felt quite at ease.

The little Princess grew up as good as she was beautiful. She knew nothing of the spell, for no one was allowed to tell her. Anyway, most people had forgotten all about it, it was so long ago.

On her fifteenth birthday, the Princess had a party and she and her friends played hide-and-seek. Away ran the Princess through the castle to find a good place to hide. In so doing, she came to a tower she had never visited before. She climbed the stairs gaily and there in a tiny room at the top she found an old, old woman twisting her thread round a *spindle*. She had lived in this far-off room for so long that she had never heard of the King's command.

At once the Princess felt that she *must* hold the spindle in her hand and she begged the old woman to give it to her.

'Very well, child,' said the old woman and gave it into her hand, for she knew no better.

The Princess took it, pricked her finger, and immediately fell to the ground in a deep sleep.

The old woman, much alarmed, fetched help but no one could do anything – the King and Queen, the doctors, the wise women – all were helpless, for the Princess was enchanted. She heard and saw nothing.

Sadly the King carried her to her room and placed her on a beautiful bed of gold and silver with hangings of rose-coloured silk and satin. Her cheeks were as pink as ever, her lips as red, her hair as golden. Then the King and Queen kissed their lovely daughter and, with tears in their eyes, they went away.

By this time, the good seventh fairy had heard what had happened. She arrived in a chariot drawn by snow-white swans. Without wasting any time she waved her wand and immediately everyone fell into as deep a sleep as the Princess – the King and Queen on their throne, the servants at their tasks, the horses in the stables, the cats and dogs and the Princess's pet doves – all fell instantly asleep. Even the fire's flames were stilled.

Then the fairy waved her wand for the last time and within a few minutes the palace and its grounds were hidden from sight by bushes and trees. So thick were they that no man might force a way through. Before long no one remembered the Princess at all, except as a story, and she slept in peace.

Years went by – fifty years, a hundred years – and a Prince came to those parts hunting the wild deer. Galloping ahead of his servants, he found himself in a wood and suddenly caught sight of the towers and battlements of a castle above the topmost branches.

'This is strange,' thought the Prince. 'I did not think anyone lived near this wood'; and calling an old woodcutter who was working near by, he asked him if he knew whose the castle was.

'I have never seen it before,' answered the old man looking at it in surprise. 'My father used to tell me that there was a castle hereabouts – he did say, too, that a beautiful Princess is asleep there waiting for a Prince to rescue her.'

'Who knows?' the Prince said. 'I may be the lucky Prince who wakens her.'

He tied up his horse and with his sword in his hand, he began to make his way through the trees towards the castle. He could now see it quite plainly, for the forest seemed to open out in front of him as he walked. There was only a narrow path and brambles and bushes were tangled on either side of it, but the Prince went on eagerly. How still it was! Not a bird sang, not a leaf rustled, and no animals watched him pass by. His own footsteps seemed the only sound in the world.

So he came out of the forest and there before him stood a fine castle. No one came out to welcome or challenge him as he entered the courtyard, but he saw that there were many people there. All of them slept. Dogs lay asleep, the horses stood motionless in their stables and even the spiders were still in their webs.

In the kitchen the servants stood without moving and the cook was holding a spoon in mid air over a bowl of batter. There was not a sound anywhere.

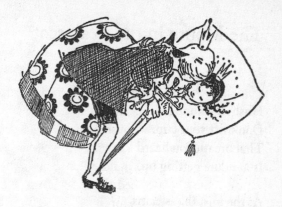

Through the silent rooms walked the Prince on tiptoe, for he feared to disturb the sleepers. He climbed a wide, marble stairway and went into a room with wide open windows. The sunshine streamed on to a bed and there lay the most beautiful girl he had ever seen. She seemed to be about fifteen or sixteen years old, her cheeks were pink, her lips red, and her golden hair was spread round her.

Leaning over the Princess, the Prince saw that she was breathing quietly. She was so young and beautiful that he could not help kissing her.

At once she awoke and sitting up she cried joyfully: 'Oh, what a lovely dream I have had!' The spell was broken!

As soon as the Princess woke, so did everyone else. The servants went on with their work, the dogs ran round barking, the horses neighed in the stables, the birds sang, and the garden blossomed into beautiful flowers of every scent and colour.

In came the King and Queen to welcome the Prince and there he stood with the Princess on his arm! Before long they were married and lived happily ever after, as well they might.

The Mouse in the Wainscot

Hush, Suzanne!
Don't lift your cup.
That breath you heard
Is a mouse getting up.

As the mist that steams
From your milk as you sup,
So soft is the sound
Of a mouse getting up.

There! did you hear
His feet pitter-patter,
Lighter than tipping
Of beads on a platter,

And then like a shower
On the window pane
The little feet scampering
Back again?

O falling of feather!
O drift of a leaf!
The mouse in the wainscot
Is dropping asleep.

IAN SERRAILLIER

Mary-Mary Earns Some Money

BY JOAN G. ROBINSON

(Mary-Mary is the youngest of five children, so her big brothers and sisters often tell her what to do and how to do it. Usually Mary-Mary does just the opposite at once!)

One day Mary-Mary saw all her big brothers and sisters coming out of the kitchen looking very busy and important. Miriam had a bucket of water and a scrubbing-brush, Martyn had a broom, Mervyn had a set of shoe-brushes, and Meg had a packet of soap powder.

'What are you all going to do?' said Mary-Mary.

'Don't worry us now,' said Miriam.

'We're busy,' said Martyn.

'We're going to do some work,' said Mervyn.

'And earn some money,' said Meg.

Mary-Mary looked at the bucket of water, the packet of soap-powder, and all the different kinds of brushes, and thought they looked interesting.

'I'll come too,' she said.

But all the others turned round together and said, 'Oh, no, Mary-Mary – not you! Now do go away.'

So, of course, Mary-Mary followed them.

Miriam went to the back-door step and began scrubbing it. Mary-Mary watched her and thought it looked rather fun to dip the brush in the bucket like that and slosh water all over the step.

'Are you going to get money for doing that?' she asked, rather surprised.

'Yes,' said Miriam. 'Threepence. When you're as big as me you'll be able to earn threepence too.'

'I'll do it now,' said Mary-Mary, reaching for the brush.

'Oh, no, you won't,' said Miriam. 'You'll upset the bucket.'

Mary-Mary stepped backwards and sat in the bucket by mistake. It upset.

'Now look what you've done,' said Miriam.

'I don't need to look,' said Mary-Mary. 'I can feel it. That water was very wet.'

Miriam went off to fill the bucket with more water, and Mary-Mary, with her skirt all wet and dripping, went away to see what the others were doing.

Martyn was sweeping up the mess round the dustbins.

'Will you get threepence for doing that?' asked Mary-Mary.

'Yes,' said Martyn, 'and so can you when you're as big as me.'

'I'll start now,' said Mary-Mary, reaching for the broom.

'No, you're not big enough,' said Martyn. 'You'd make yourself dirty.'

Mary-Mary stepped backwards and tripped over a pile of dust and tea-leaves. It flew up all round her, and as she was wet it stuck to her in quite a few places.

'I seem to have got rather dirty,' she said.

'I knew you would,' said Martyn, and he started sweeping it up all over again.

So Mary-Mary, with her skirt all wet and dripping, and covered with dust and tea-leaves, went away to see what the others were doing.

Mervyn was kneeling on the garden step polishing shoes. Mary-Mary stood and watched for a while. Two tins of polish lay open on the step, one very black and one shiny brown. Mervyn dipped one brush into the polish and put it on the shoes, then he rubbed them with another brush and polished them with a soft cloth until they shone.

'Do you like doing that?' asked Mary-Mary.

'Not much,' said Mervyn, 'but I'll get threepence for it.'

Mary-Mary knelt down on the step beside him.

'Now I'll do some,' she said.

'No, you won't,' said Mervyn. 'You'll only get covered in polish. Get up, now.'

Mary-Mary got up, and the two tins of polish were stuck to her knees. She hadn't looked where she was kneeling, and the very black one was stuck to her right knee, and the shiny brown one was stuck to her left knee. She took them off quickly before Mervyn noticed. He was polishing hard.

'When you're as big as me, you'll be able to earn threepence, too,' he said. 'Now do go away. You'll only get covered in polish.'

Mary-Mary looked at her knees.

'I am already,' she said, and rubbed some of it off on to her hands.

So Mary-Mary, with her skirt all wet and dripping, covered with dust and tea-leaves, and with shoe polish on her hands and knees, went away to see what Meg was doing.

Meg was in the garden washing her dolls' blankets in a bowl.

'Why are you doing that?' said Mary-Mary.

'They were very dirty,' said Meg, 'and if I wash all the dolls' clothes as well I'm going to get threepence.'

Mary-Mary picked up the packet of soap powder.

'I'll do some washing too,' she said. 'I'd like to earn three-pence.'

'You can't,' said Meg. 'You're too little. Wait till you're as big as me and then you can. Put down that packet – you'll spill it.'

But Mary-Mary held the packet high above her head and wouldn't put it down.

'You're spilling it!' shouted Meg. 'You've got it upside down. It's running all over your hair.'

Mary-Mary put it down again.

'I wondered what was tickling my head,' she said.

'Go away now,' said Meg.

'No,' said Mary-Mary, and stayed where she was.

'Oh, well, then – stay if you must,' said Meg.

'No, I won't,' said Mary-Mary. 'I'm going away.'

So Mary-Mary, with her skirt all wet and dripping, covered with dust and tea-leaves, with shoe-polish on her hands and knees, and soap powder all over her head, went round to the front gate to see if anyone else might be doing anything interesting.

A cat was sitting washing itself on the wall outside. Mary-Mary opened the gate, stroked the cat, and looked around.

The coal cart was standing a few doors away, outside Mr

Bassett's house. The coalman wasn't there, but Mr Bassett was walking round and round the cart talking to himself. Every now and then he stooped down and tried to look underneath it, but he was a big, fat man, and it was difficult for him to bend easily in the middle.

Mary-Mary wondered what he was doing, and who he was talking to. The coalman's horse was eating out of a nose bag and didn't seem to be taking any notice of him.

Mary-Mary moved a little nearer.

Mr Bassett straightened his back, looked at the horse with a worried face, and said, 'Puss, puss.'

'It isn't a cat. It's a horse,' said Mary-Mary.

Mr Bassett turned and saw her.

'Ah, Mary-Mary!' he said. 'You're a much better size than I am. Do you mind looking under the coal cart and telling me what you can see there?'

Mary-Mary bent down.

'I can see a lump of coal,' she said.

'Anything else?' asked Mr Bassett.

'Yes,' said Mary-Mary, 'quite a lot of things. There's another lump of coal and a silver pencil and a piece of paper –'

'Isn't there a cat there?' asked Mr Bassett.

'No,' said Mary-Mary.

'Are you quite sure?' said Mr Bassett.

'Yes, quite sure,' said Mary-Mary, 'but there's a cat sitting on the wall over there if you really want one.'

Mr Bassett looked up and saw the cat washing itself on the wall.

'Well, I never!' he said. 'It must have run out when I wasn't looking. I saw it go under the cart as I came out of the gate, and I was afraid it might get run over when the coalman came

back. I bent down to call it out, but it wouldn't come back. Then I felt something fall out of my pocket, but I was more worried about the cat.'

Mary-Mary liked Mr Bassett. It was kind of him to be so worried about the cat.

'Shall I fetch out what you dropped?' she asked. 'I can get under the cart more easily than you can.'

'Won't you get dirty?'

Mary-Mary looked down at herself.

'I don't think I could get much dirtier than I am,' she said.

'No, perhaps not,' said Mr Bassett. 'It's very kind of you.'

So Mary-Mary crawled underneath the back of the coal cart, and Mr Bassett stood by waiting.

'Oh!' called Mary-Mary, 'there's half a crown down here as well!'

'Good,' said Mr Bassett. 'Bring out everything you see. I can't be quite sure what fell out of my pocket.'

So Mary-Mary picked up the half-crown and the two lumps of coal and the piece of paper and the silver pencil, and crawled out again.

'Good girl,' said Mr Bassett. 'Now let's sort them out. These two lumps of coal belong to the coalman, so we'll throw them back on the cart, and the silver pencil belongs to me, so I'll put it in my pocket. The paper doesn't belong to anybody, so we'll throw it away, and the half-crown – well – I think the half-crown belongs to you, because you've earned it.'

'How did I earn it?' asked Mary-Mary.

'By being just the size to fetch it out,' said Mr Bassett. 'What would you like to spend it on?'

Mary-Mary said, 'I've been thinking all the morning that if I had threepence I'd spend it on an ice lolly.'

Mr Bassett began counting on his fingers.

'We could buy ten ice lollies with this half-crown,' he said, 'but I think that's too many, don't you? Let's go and spend it, anyway. Shall we go to that nice little teashop on the corner?'

'Oh, yes,' said Mary-Mary. 'I'd like to go there very much. That's where I go to watch the ladies sitting in the window drinking their coffee. It's next to the lolly shop. I've always wanted to look like one of those ladies.'

'Very well,' said Mr Bassett, 'so you shall.'

Mary-Mary looked down at herself.

'I'm rather dirty to look like a lady,' she said.

'And I'm rather fat, and don't look like a lady, either,' said Mr Bassett. 'But if we feel right and behave right I don't suppose anyone will notice what we look like. You don't shout and throw things about, do you?'

'Not usually,' said Mary-Mary.

'Or lick your plate?'

'Not when I'm out,' said Mary-Mary.

'Nor do I,' said Mr Bassett, 'so we ought to be all right.'

So Mary-Mary with her skirt still damp, decorated with dust and tea-leaves, with shoe-polish on her hands and knees, soap powder all over her hair, and a smudge of coal-dust on the end of her nose, went walking politely down the road with Mr Bassett to the nice little teashop.

'We will order one very large ice-cream sundae, and one cup of tea,' said Mr Bassett.

'Which will be for which?' asked Mary-Mary politely.

'I shall order the ice-cream sundae for myself,' said Mr Bassett, 'because I like ice-cream sundaes very much. But I am not allowed to eat them, because they make me too fat, so you shall eat it for me and I shall watch you.'

87

'I don't like tea very much,' said Mary-Mary.

'Then I shall drink it for you,' said Mr Bassett, 'and we shall suit each other very nicely.'

From *Mary-Mary*

The Easter Lamb

BY MARGARET GORE

It was Spring – Spring in Italy. The sun shone yellow on the fruit ripening in the lemon and orange groves, the flowers opened their petals to the new warmth – and the little curly white lamb skipped. He did not know it was Spring; he only knew he loved to skip. He was happy doing nothing but this all day long, springing and bouncing like a soft, white ball. At last even he grew tired; he lay down and watched the white, fleecy clouds which sometimes floated across the blue sky. He wondered whether they were lambs, too.

Every day the shepherd, Dominic, came up from the little village to tend the sheep. Dominic was a fine young man, tanned brown by the hot sun. He laughed a lot and when he laughed his teeth showed white against his brown skin. In the Summertime he used to sit for hours on the hillside, watching the sheep and playing on his pipe. Then the little lamb would come up quite close to Dominic and stare at him with big,

89

round eyes. The shepherd was fond of the little white lamb, and he would stop playing, put down his pipe, and hold out his hand to the lamb.

'Come,' he would say, in the deep, kindly voice which the little lamb was beginning to know so well. 'Come, I am your friend, come.'

Then the little lamb would come closer timidly, until he was near enough to sniff at the tips of the shepherd's fingers.

'There, that's right,' said Dominic. 'There's nothing to be afraid of, you see,' and he would gently tickle the top of the lamb's curly head with his brown fingers.

One day, while Dominic was up on the hillside, the bells rang out from the great church in the village. The little lamb wondered why they were ringing and Dominic told him. Not that he really understood, but Dominic always talked to him, perhaps because there was no one but the sheep to talk to up on the hills, anyway.

'That's the bellringers practising,' he said. 'They're getting ready for Easter Day.'

'Easter Day? Easter Day?' It meant nothing to the little lamb. 'Oh well,' he said and skipped lightly away.

Next day some children came up to play on the hillside, as they often did. They, too, began to talk about Easter Day – of what they would do, and what they would wear, and how they would get up very early in the morning. The little lamb wanted to know more about Easter Day. He came up close and gave a little *baa-baa*, but the children only laughed and tried to stroke him and he backed away again.

When the children went home, however, the lamb decided to follow them. So, for the first time in his life, he left the hills and trotted down the steep, dusty road to the village. One by one the children ran off home, and at last the lamb was left all by himself in the narrow village street. *Plock-plock* went his tiny hooves on the shiny cobblestones, and *sniff-sniff* went his nose, smelling at everything. To tell the truth, he was half curious and half afraid.

It was a very pretty village. Flowers hung down from the balconies of the houses. The road was very hot, but here and there he saw shady courtyards, with trees making cool purple and yellow splashes. A hen came strutting out across the road, clucking to herself. The lamb stared at her; she took no notice of him, however, but boldly walked through a gap in the fence and into a garden.

The lamb was beginning to enjoy himself, and he skipped off down the road to see what else there was to be seen.

As he passed one of the little white houses, he smelt a delicious spicy smell. 'Whatever is that lovely smell?' thought the lamb. 'What can it be?'

He poked his curly head round the doorway. Inside was a woman with dark hair and golden ear-rings. She smiled when she saw the little lamb and shook her apron at him.

'Shoo, little lamb, shoo! I am busy baking my Easter buns and then I must bake the Easter cake for all my children. Shoo, shoo!'

'Easter cake? Easter buns?' The little lamb did not understand at all. 'Oh well,' he said and danced away down the street.

He came now to a big, grey, stone building. The little lamb knew what it was. He knew it from the big shining cross on top, which he could see from his home up on the hillside. It was from here that he had heard the bellringers practising. Every day, too, the bells rang out three times – in the morning, at

midday, and in the evening. On Sundays the bells rang a great
many times and Dominic, the shepherd, put on his best clothes
and went to church.

Today, the church was quiet. The little lamb climbed carefully up the steps – his hooves clattering a little on the hard
stone – right up to the great door. He poked his black nose
inquisitively inside.

There he saw a little band of women with scarves over their
heads. They were kneeling down, but they were not saying
their prayers. They had buckets of water and big, floppy cloths,
and they were all scrubbing as hard as ever they could.

'Baa-baa! Whatever's going on here?' asked the lamb.

One of the women looked up when she heard his voice.

'Look,' she called to her companions, 'here's a lamb trying to
come in. Run away, little lamb, we're very busy. We have the
whole church to scrub before Easter Day. Everything must be
spotlessly clean for Easter Day!'

The woman shook her cloth at the little lamb, and he lost no
time in skipping nimbly down the church steps and away.

He wondered very much why everything must be spotlessly clean for Easter Day. Sadly he looked down at his own little hooves, which were rather black because only that morning he had jumped in some muddy water up in the hills.

'Meeh!' he bleated. 'What can *I* do for Easter Day?'

By this time, his four muddy paws had brought him into the market square. It was full of people and there were stalls of every description. Over each stall was a gay, striped cloth, which helped to keep out both the rain and the sun.

There was a big crowd of people in front of one of the stalls where a man was selling coloured eggs. 'Easter eggs! Easter eggs!' he was shouting. 'Buy your Easter eggs here!'

The lamb thought the eggs very beautiful in their blue, gold, and silver papers.

Next door to this stall was an enormous basket filled with flowers of every kind and colour. A fat, kindly old lady sat beside the basket with a big red umbrella over her head. At her feet in the shade of the umbrella sprawled a sleepy, black cat.

The little lamb edged nearer to the basket and sniffed daintily. He loved flowers.

'Flowers for Easter Day,' cried the old lady. 'Buy your flowers for Easter Day!'

At first she was too busy to notice the lamb, but, when she did see him, she smiled and said to her customers, 'Look, here's the Easter lamb!' Then she said to the lamb, 'You'd better run home, little lamb, before you get lost! Run along, now.'

The little lamb did as he was told and trotted back home up the steep hill. What had the old lady meant when she called him 'the Easter lamb'?

'Meeh,' he bleated, '*I* want to be ready for Easter Day, too.'

Easter Day came the very next day. Early in the morning,

when the first bells were ringing from the church tower, Dominic the shepherd came up the hill dressed in his best clothes, and behind him came a band of children.

To the lamb's surprise they led him down to the village, down the steep, narrow street, and into a small courtyard where some other children were waiting. All the children were dressed in their best: the boys had silk sashes and the girls wore white dresses and white veils trimmed with flowers. They made a great fuss of the little lamb – he was quite bewildered with it all. First of all, they brushed all the mud off his hooves. He was very pleased at that. Then they hung a garland of flowers about his neck.

'Oh, isn't he pretty! How sweet he looks!' chorused the girls

and boys. One little girl whispered in his ear, 'Now you are all ready for Easter Day.'

They put blue ribbons round his neck and four of them held the long ends of the ribbons in their hands to guide him. With the lamb at the front, they set off in procession for the church, walking very slowly and sedately. The lamb walked sedately too; for once he did not skip or jump at all.

So they passed through the market square towards the church as the bells pealed out their joyous Easter message.

'Meeh!' said the little lamb. 'Today is Easter Day and *I* am an Easter lamb!'

He was the proudest little lamb in all the world.

Pyp Goes to the Country

Pyp was a smart little blue car who lived in London. His cousin,
Emily, a green car, had gone to live in the country.

One day Pyp started out with his mistress to spend a holiday
with Emily. He ran along the wide main roads feeling proud
of his shining blue enamel and glittering chromium and clean
windows.

Every now and then he played his favourite game of passing
lorries. He watched carefully for a safe gap in the traffic and
then – zip! – he slipped past a lumbering lorry singing:

> 'Speeding down the highways,
>   Past the lorries – Zip!
> Running down the byways,
>   Here comes PYP.'

In two hours he was in the country and soon he drew up at
the gate of a cottage. 'Pip! Pip!' he hooted. 'Pip!' answered

his cousin Emily. She was looking out of her garage eagerly. 'Welcome to the country!' she said. She was rather shy because she was smaller and younger than Pyp.

That night Pyp was given half the garage to sleep in, so he and Emily had a chat.

'Do you like living in the country?' he asked.

'I felt dull at first,' said Emily, 'but now I like it.'

'Does anything exciting ever happen'

'There are some horrid monsters called tractors on the road,' said Emily. 'You wait until you see them! They are more like ugly animals than respectable cars.'

'I must say I'm looking forward to being here,' said Pyp, yawning. 'It will be nice and restful, I expect.'

The next day both Pyp and Emily set out together, carrying grown-ups and children for a picnic. Two little girls climbed into Pyp's back seat with iced lollies in their hands.

'I hope they know how to behave,' thought Pyp. 'I don't want my seats sticky and messy!'

The roads were rather narrow and Pyp was surprised that there were no paths and no pedestrian crossings. He didn't like people walking in the roads – roads belonged to cars.

Emily led the way. She seemed to travel very slowly. 'Hurry up, hurry up!' called Pyp. 'There's no traffic – we could speed here.'

But Emily took no notice.

There was a sudden sharp bend in the winding road and Emily disappeared round it. Pyp dashed after her too quickly and nearly skidded. The children screamed, the brakes shrieked, and Pyp stopped just in time behind Emily. In front of her was a huge, noisy monster, with queer arms and knobs and wheels all over it.

There was a lot of shouting, the children watched eagerly, and Emily waited quietly. Pyp was quiet too for he was rather ashamed of himself. Perhaps Emily knew best how to behave in the country!

Very very slowly, the monster ran into the side of the road. Its enormous wheels made deep ruts in the grass. The driver held it there and signalled to the two little cars to come on. Slowly and carefully, Emily and Pyp edged past, while everyone held their breath.

'I'm glad to see these monsters have the good manners to get out of our way,' said Pyp sharply.

Soon the cars turned off the road into a field. This was the place for the picnic. They were given a drink of water, for their radiators were rather hot, then the grown-ups and children sat down to eat their picnic. Soon the children ran off to play and the two little cars were left in peace.

The long grass stood round their wheels and rustled in the warm wind and presently the children came running back with daisy-chains to hang round the bonnets of the cars. Emily was pleased, but Pyp didn't like it much. 'Whoever heard of a car wearing flowers!' he grumbled.

98

'Don't you like being here?' asked Emily. 'The grass is nice and soft. I like it for a change.'

'*I* don't,' said Pyp crossly. 'Give me a good hard road any day.'

But soon both the cars slept in the sunshine until it was time to go home.

Next day Pyp was taken out alone. He felt in a much better temper for he had had a good rest. Besides the country was not as dull as he expected.

'I wonder what we shall meet today?' he wondered. 'Some more strange creatures perhaps.'

They did too!

As Pyp ran gaily along the winding road, he suddenly saw a strange sight on the road ahead. He pulled up so suddenly that his mistress nearly bumped her head. He was quite frightened! Right in front of him were several large black and white animals. They pushed each other and made strange noises, not a bit like a car.

'Why don't these creatures keep to their own side of the road?' said Pyp indignantly, but the animals took no notice. Waving their tails, they stared at him with their big brown eyes and went on chewing their dinner. One actually came and licked Pyp's window. 'What cheek!' said Pyp.

A man came up. 'Coo-up!' he called, and a dog ran along the road and barked at the animals' legs. Away they ran clumsily and turned into a farm gate. The road was clear once more.

The sun had been shining all morning, but now black clouds gathered and rain began to fall. Soon there were big puddles on the road. Splash! Bump! Splash! Bump! went Pyp. 'Oh dear, how dirty I shall be!' he thought in dismay.

He struggled along through the rain and the mud, until suddenly a milk-lorry backed out of a field in front of him. It rocked and swayed on to the road and, just as it passed Pyp, its wheels went right through a deep puddle. Splash went the muddy water all over Pyp's side-windows and bonnet! The little car gasped for breath and couldn't see at all. His mistress had to get out and wipe his windows before he could go on again.

Grumbling to himself, Pyp went on and turned into a lane so narrow that there was hardly room for him at all. He couldn't turn round again either.

Ting-a-ling went a bicycle bell and a boy rushed round the corner. Pyp drew into the hedge so quickly that the thorny bushes scratched his enamel, his wheels squelched in the thick mud, and a branch scraped his roof. Poor Pyp! How glad he was when a little while later, he ran into the dry garage where Emily was waiting.

'See what a mess I'm in!' he complained. 'Someone must wash me before I go to sleep.'

'Oh, don't fuss,' said Emily. 'Often I have to stay for days with dirty wheels and windows. Country roads are muddy because of the farms and fields.'

'Horrible!' said Pyp, shuddering. 'I hate to be dirty. I don't think I like the country.'

'I do,' said Emily firmly. 'It's much nicer than your smelly London.'

Next day was Pyp's last day in the country. It was a fine sunny day and he quite enjoyed it. He was on his way back to Emily when he suddenly felt very tired indeed.

'There's something wrong inside my bonnet!' he exclaimed – and stopped dead.

His mistress tried to start him up again. 'Come on, Pyp,' she said kindly. 'Do your best.'

But it was no good. She had to go to a near-by garage and fetch someone to see what was wrong.

The man looked at the plugs. 'A-aah,' he said. 'There's dirt in here, that's what.'

He cleaned them out and started up Pyp's engine. Pyp groaned, for it hurt his inside, but soon – *prr-rr-rr* – he felt quite well again.

'Dirt inside as well as out now!' he said to himself. 'Thank goodness we go home tomorrow.'

Early next morning, Pyp and his mistress started home. 'Good-bye, Emily,' he called. 'I'm sorry I was so cross. You must come and see us in London.'

Away sped the little car along the wide main roads, singing:

'Speeding down the highways,
Past the lorries – Zip!
Running down the byways,
Here comes PYP.'

Cars swished behind and in front of him and Pyp was happy. And here was his own garage. His engine stopped and he sighed with pleasure. 'Tomorrow someone will clean me and I shall see lots of traffic,' he said sleepily. 'London for me!' and he fell asleep.

Noise, by Pooh

Oh, the honey-bees are gumming
On their little wings, and humming
That the summer, which is coming,
  Will be fun.
And the cows are almost cooing,
And the turtle-doves are mooing,
Which is why a Pooh is poohing
  In the sun.

For the spring is really springing;
You can see a skylark singing,
And the blue-bells, which are ringing,
  Can be heard.
And the cuckoo isn't cooing,
But he's cucking and he's ooing,
And a Pooh is simply poohing
  Like a bird.

A. A. MILNE From *The House at Pooh Corner*

Mrs Pepperpot and the Moose

BY ALF PRØYSEN

It was winter-time, and Mrs Pepperpot was having trouble getting water. The tap in her kitchen ran slower and slower, until one day it just dripped and then stopped altogether. The well was empty.

'Ah, well,' thought Mrs Pepperpot, 'it won't be the first time I've had this kind of trouble, and it won't be the last. But with two strong arms and a good sound bucket, not to mention the lucky chance that there's another well down by the forest fence, we'll soon fix that.'

So she put on her husband's old winter coat and a pair of thick gloves and fetched a pickaxe from the woodshed. Then she trudged through the snow down the hill, to where there was a dip by the forest fence. She swept the snow away and started breaking a hole in the ice with the pickaxe. Chips of ice flew

everywhere as Mrs Pepperpot hacked away, not looking to left or right. She made such a noise that she never heard the sound of breaking twigs, nor the snorting that was coming from the other side of the fence.

But there he was; a huge moose with great big antlers, not moving at all, but staring angrily at Mrs Pepperpot. Suddenly he gave a very loud snort and leaped over the fence, butting Mrs Pepperpot from behind, so that she went head-first into a pile of snow!

'What the dickens!' cried Mrs Pepperpot as she scrambled to her feet. But by that time the moose was back on the other side of the fence. When she saw what it was that had pushed her over, Mrs Pepperpot lost no time in scrambling up the hill and into her house, locking the door behind her. Then she peeped out of the kitchen window to see if the moose was still there. He was.

'You wait, you great big brute!' said Mrs Pepperpot. 'I'll give you a fright you won't forget!'

She put on a black rain-cape and a battered old hat, and in her hand she carried a big stick. Then she crept out of the door and hid round the corner of the house.

The moose was quietly nibbling the bark off the trees and seemed to be taking no notice of her.

Suddenly she stormed down the hill, shouting, 'Woollah, Woollah, Woollah!' like a Red Indian, the black rain-cape flapping round her and the stick waving in the air. The moose *should* have been frightened, but he just took one look at the whirling thing coming towards him, leaped the fence, and headed straight for it!

Poor Mrs Pepperpot! All she could do was to rush back indoors again as fast as she knew how.

'Now what shall I do?' she wondered. 'I must have water to cook my potatoes and do my washing-up, and a little cup of coffee wouldn't come amiss after all this excitement. Perhaps if I were to put on my old man's trousers and take his gun out ... I could pretend to aim it; that might scare him off.'

So she put on the trousers and took out the gun; but this was the silliest idea she had had yet, because, before she was half-way down the hill, that moose came pounding towards her on his great long legs. She never had time to point the gun. Worse still, she dropped it in her efforts to keep the trousers up and run back to the house at the same time. When the moose saw her disappear indoors, he turned and stalked down the hill again, but this time he didn't jump back over the fence, but stayed by the well, as if he were guarding it.

'Ah well,' said Mrs Pepperpot, 'I suppose I shall have to fill the bucket with snow and melt it to get the water I need. That moose is clearly not afraid of anything.'

So she took her bucket and went outside. But just as she was bending down to scoop up the snow, she turned small! But this time the magic worked quicker than usual, and somehow she managed to tumble into the bucket which was lying on its side. The bucket started to roll down the hill; faster and faster it went, and poor Mrs Pepperpot was seeing stars as she bumped round and round inside.

Just above the dip near the well a little mound jutted out, and here the bucket made a leap into space. 'This is the end of me!' thought Mrs Pepperpot. She waited for the bump, but it didn't come! Instead the bucket seemed to be floating through the air, over the fence, and right into the forest. If she had had time to think, Mrs Pepperpot would have known that the moose had somehow caught the bucket on one of his antlers, but it is not so

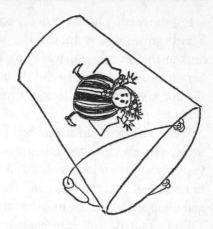

easy to think when you're swinging between heaven and earth.

At last the bucket got stuck on a branch and the moose thundered on through the undergrowth. Mrs Pepperpot lay there panting, trying to get her breath back. She had no idea where she was. But then she heard: 'Chuck, chuck! Chuck, chuck!' – the chattering of a squirrel as he ran down the tree-trunk over her head.

'Hullo!' said the squirrel, 'if it isn't Mrs Pepperpot. Out for a walk, or something?'

'Not exactly a *walk*,' said Mrs Pepperpot, 'but I've had a free ride, though I don't know who gave it to me.'

'That was the King of the Moose,' said the squirrel. 'I saw him gallop past with a wild look in his eyes. It's the first time I have ever seen him afraid, I can tell you that. He is so stupid and so stuck-up you wouldn't believe it. All he thinks of is fighting; he goes for anything and anybody – the bigger the better. But you seem to have given him the fright of his life.'

'I'm glad I managed it in the end,' said Mrs Pepperpot, 'and now I'd be gladder still if I knew how to get myself home.'

107

But she needn't have worried, because at that moment she felt herself grow large again, and the next thing she knew she had broken the branch and was lying on the ground. She picked herself and her bucket up and started walking home. But when she got to the fence she took a turn down to the well to fill the bucket.

When she stood up she looked back towards the forest, and there, sure enough, stood the moose, blinking at her. But Mrs Pepperpot was no longer afraid of him. All she had to do was to rattle that bucket a little, and the big creature shook his head and disappeared silently into the forest.

From that day on Mrs Pepperpot had no trouble fetching water from the well by the forest fence.

From *Mrs Pepperpot Again*

Puss-in-Boots

TRADITIONAL

Once upon a time there was a miller who had three sons. When he died he left the mill to one, his donkey to the second, and his cat to the youngest son, Jack.

Now Jack was fond of Puss, but a cat is not much help in earning a living. 'What are we going to do, Puss?' asked Jack sadly, stroking the cat gently.

To his astonishment Puss answered: 'Don't despair, Jack! If you will buy me a pair of boots, a hat, and a bag, maybe I can help you to make your fortune.'

'I never knew you could speak, Puss!' exclaimed Jack. 'Now we can be better friends than ever. I promise to buy whatever you need, even if it takes my last penny.'

So Jack bought Puss a pair of riding-boots, a hat with a tall, curling feather, and a bag. Very handsome he looked in them too, for he was a good-looking cat with fine whiskers.

That night Jack and his cat sheltered in an old cottage at the gate of a park belonging to a wicked giant. Early next morning, Puss put on his boots and hat, went into the giant's park, and caught two fat rabbits in his bag. Then he hurried to the palace and demanded to see the King. At first the servants would not let him in, but Puss looked so fine and talked so well that they agreed to take him in to the King.

Puss bowed and said: 'Your Majesty, my master sends you these rabbits with his humble greetings.'

'Pray thank him on my behalf,' said the King. 'But who is your master and how does he come to have a cat as a servant?'

'My master is the noble Marquis of Carabas,' replied Puss. 'All his servants are invisible except me. It is the custom in my master's family to have a cat as Prime Minister.'

The King gave him a bag of gold for the Marquis and at once Puss hurried to the town and bought food for himself and his master, so that they feasted royally.

The next morning, Puss caught two fat partridges in his bag and took them to the King with the same message. This time the King called his daughter, the Princess, to see the talking cat. When he left the King gave him not only a bag of diamonds but a red ribbon to tie round his neck. 'You must ask your master to come and see me,' he said.

'Puss!' exclaimed the miller's son, 'What will happen? You know I cannot go to see the King. I have no fine clothes or money to buy them with.'

Next day the cat heard the King tell the Princess that he

would take her for a drive by the river. Away he ran to his master. 'You have only to bathe in the river at a place I shall show you, Master,' he cried, 'and your fortune will be made.'

The miller's son could not refuse his dear cat, so he got into the river. Without saying anything to him, Puss hid his master's clothes under a stone.

When he saw the King's carriage approaching, Puss ran out into the road and cried loudly: 'Help! Help! My master, the Marquis of Carabas, is drowning!'

As soon as the King recognized Puss-in-Boots, he sent his men to rescue Jack. But the boy's clothes could not be found, so the King had to lend him a fine suit of silk and satin. He looked so handsome in these magnificent clothes that he was invited to drive with the King and his daughter in the royal carriage.

Puss hurried to a large field where farm hands were gathering in the harvest. 'When the King asks you who owns these fields, you must say that they belong to the Marquis of Carabas,' he said fiercely, 'or you will be chopped into mincemeat!'

The men were so frightened of this fierce cat in boots who could talk, that they agreed and when the King drove up and remarked what fine fields these were, they cried: 'They belong to the Marquis of Carabas.'

Meanwhile Puss ran on until he came to some shepherds with a fine flock of sheep. 'If the King asks you to whom these sheep belong you must say "To the Marquis of Carabas",' he said fiercely, 'or you will be chopped into mincemeat.'

When the King came by, the frightened shepherds cried: 'These flocks belong to the noble Marquis of Carabas.'

Farther on, woodcutters and gamekeepers were working in the woods. 'When the King asks you about these woods, you must say they belong to the Marquis of Carabas,' said the cat fiercely, 'or you will be chopped into mincemeat.'

The woodcutters and gamekeepers were terrified of this fierce talking cat, so they told the King that the woods belonged to the Marquis of Carabas.

The king was delighted to hear that the Marquis was so rich. 'It is strange,' he said, 'but I thought all the land round here belonged to a wicked giant. I am glad it all belongs to you, my friend!'

The miller's son did not know what to say, so he left it to his clever cat to arrange matters for him.

Puss had run on with the speed of the wind and had reached the giant's castle. He rang the bell boldly and the giant himself came to the door. When he saw the tiny person in boots and a plumed hat, he was astonished.

'What do you want?' he roared.

'I am Puss-in-Boots, Prime Minister to the Marquis of Cara-bas and the favourite of the King of the Cannibal Islands,' said Puss bravely.

'The King of the Cannibal Islands is my cousin,' said the giant a little more pleasantly. 'Come in, whipper-snapper.'

The cat saw that the castle was a most magnificent place, full of treasures and costly furnishings. Just the thing for the Marquis of Carabas.

Puss bowed to the ground. 'Is it true, your highness, that you can turn yourself into any large animal you please?' he asked.

'I can, O Cat,' said the giant. 'Would you like to see me do it?' And in the twinkling of an eye, he turned himself into an enormous elephant.

'Wonderful!' cried Puss.

'That's nothing,' said the giant proudly and changed into a lion.

Puss was very frightened. He climbed up to the beams in the roof and would not come down again until the giant had turned himself back into his human shape.

'Marvellous!' he said. 'But I am sure you could not turn yourself into a really *small* animal, a dog or a mouse?'

'You shall see, you shall see!' boasted the giant.

At once he turned into a dog and ran after Puss. Then he became a rat, and then a mouse. With one blow of his paw, Puss-in-Boots killed the mouse and that was the end of the giant.

At this very moment, the King's carriage arrived. Puss ran out and bowing cried: 'Welcome to the castle of my lord, the Marquis of Carabas!'

The King and the Princess and Jack walked into the great hall and there was a fine feast spread out on the table, enough for two giants.

'You must excuse this small meal,' said the cat. 'We did not know that the King would honour us for dinner.'

They all sat down and feasted – Puss as well – and then went over the giant's castle. It was indeed magnificent. Puss went before them bowing and pointing out his master's fine new possessions. Jack followed with the beautiful Princess on his arm. 'What a wonderful Puss I have!' he said over and over again.

'If you would like to marry my daughter,' said the King, 'I shall be pleased to give my consent, for I can see that you are rich and well-bred.'

'First I must tell you the truth,' said Jack, for he was an honest boy. He told the King the whole story of how Puss had gained him lands and a castle. The King laughed till he cried.

'Oh, what a wonderful cat!' he cried. 'I will make him my

Prime Minister for I am sure I shall never find a better or more clever. And you, Jack, shall really be the Marquis of Carabas from this moment.'

So the miller's son married the Princess and they lived happily ever after. And so did their good friend Puss-in-Boots, Prime Minister and friend of the King of the Cannibal Islands.

David's First Flight

BY UNA NORRIS

David was feeling very excited. Not only was he going to spend his summer holiday with Aunty Vina who lived in Switzerland, but he was flying there by aeroplane – all by himself, too!

Mummy and Daddy had come to the airport to see him off. They were all standing in the big hall, with crowds of other people. What a hubbub there was! From outside came the scream of jets landing and taking off and the roar of engines. David longed to watch them but there were big buildings in the way. Presently he would be able to see the planes properly, for the air-hostess, who was going to look after him on the journey, would take him through the barrier.

Only one thing made him feel sad. A few weeks ago – on his sixth birthday – Daddy had given him a lively black puppy for his very own. They were such friends, and David took Sooty everywhere; so, of course, he thought Sooty could go with him to Switzerland. He was very disappointed when Daddy explained that you were not allowed to take pet animals on board an aeroplane. 'You see,' he said, 'a little dog might get frightened and that would cause trouble.' So now David was holding Sooty in his arms, giving him a last hug, as the time drew near for leaving him.

Slung over David's shoulder was his blue canvas hold-all, with the air company's name in white letters, so everyone would know he was going by aeroplane. He felt very important, because inside was his 'passport' and without it, Daddy told him, he would not be allowed to go into Switzerland, so he must be very, very careful not to lose it.

'Hello! What a dear little puppy!' A smiling young woman in a smart blue uniform gave Sooty a friendly pat. 'I'm your air-hostess, Miss Green.'

'This is David,' said Daddy. 'I hope he won't be any trouble.'

Just then a giant voice boomed out. 'Will passengers for Flight Number 234, please go to the passport office.'

'That means us, David,' said Miss Green. 'Say good-bye now.'

'Good-bye, Sooty.' David rubbed his cheek against the puppy's cold moist nose, while Sooty licked his face all over. 'Good-bye, Mummy. Good-bye, Daddy.'

'We'll take great care of Sooty,' promised Mother. 'He'll be waiting for you when you get back.'

'Come along, David,' called Miss Green. 'We'll see about your passport and then I'll take you straight out to the plane.'

At last David could really see the landing ground. There were planes everywhere, standing on the tarmac, circling in the sky, or gliding in to land. How big they were! Ever so much bigger than they looked when passing over the garden at home. In no time he was seated in a jeep between the driver and Miss Green. Fancy being *driven* out to the plane! 'We'll race all the other passengers and be first on board,' smiled the air hostess. How exciting it all was!

'Look David! That's our plane over there!' said Miss Green. 'The one with the red wings and the red square on its tail. That's the Viscount.'

David thought it looked like a great fish with a pointed nose and a row of eyes all along the side of its body. 'What's that lorry-thing doing underneath it?' he asked curiously.

'That's all the luggage going in through a hole in the tail,' said the driver, pulling up with a jerk. 'Look slippy, young fellow! Here we are!'

And now David could see a big yellow gangway on wheels stretched from the ground up to a small doorway into the plane. Looking up, it seemed quite a long way above him as he began to climb the steps.

'We're *not* the first on board like you said, Miss Green,' he said accusingly, stopping suddenly. At the entrance to the plane, watching him, was a fair-haired boy of about ten.

'Why, it's Michael! Are you coming with us this trip?' called Miss Green.

'Yes, all the way!' grinned Michael.

The air-hostess turned to David. 'You're in luck!' she said.

'Michael is the son of our pilot. He'll tell you all you want to know.'

'Hello!' said Michael, holding out a friendly hand. 'Let's sit together.' Feeling rather shy, but very happy, David stepped through the little doorway and followed his new friend into the plane.

Inside, the passengers' cabin was like a super-bus with lots of windows and deep cushioned seats down each side. 'Here you are, two front seats,' smiled Miss Green.

'You can have the window,' offered Michael to David's delight.

The other passengers began to climb aboard. 'We won't be long now,' said Miss Green. 'What about a sweet? You can have two each as a special treat.'

'Ooh, goody!' exclaimed David. 'Fancy getting toffees, too!'

'It helps when you take off or land,' explained Michael. 'It stops your ears popping.'

'How can ears pop! How funny it sounds!' said David and the two boys rocked with laughter.

In a few minutes a voice said, 'Fasten your belts, and no smoking, please.'

'That's Dad speaking over the inter-com,' whispered Michael. 'Everyone has to do just what he says, because he's the captain, just like on a ship.' The same notice flashed on a screen. David felt very proud of himself because he could read the word 'Belts' for himself.

'This is how it goes, see?' said Michael, snapping his own safety-catch into place and then giving David a hand with his.

'We're moving!' cried David excitedly, as the plane taxied along the tarmac. 'Oh, it's stopped!'

'That's all right,' said Michael. 'We've got to turn into the wind before we take off.'

A terrific roaring now began as the powerful engines 'revved up'. The whole plane seemed to shiver and shake with the vibration. David watched the propellers begin to turn, slowly at first, then faster and faster until he could hardly see them. The plane was moving along the runway now, gathering speed. Suddenly looking down David saw the airfield dropping away beneath them – buildings, houses, and green fields getting smaller and smaller. 'Hurrah! We're up!' he shouted, quite forgetting where he was in his excitement, and taking no notice of Michael's correction, 'It's called being airborne.' It was a lovely floating feeling. You hardly knew you were moving, except for the steady drone of the engines. Higher and higher they rose, and now they were right among the clouds, thousands of feet up in the sky. 'We must be nearly up to the moon,' thought David.

'I do hope we run into a thunderstorm,' Michael said cheerfully. 'That would be something if you like.'

'Oh, yes,' echoed David bravely, though he wasn't quite sure that he really *did* want a storm.

David spotted a large envelope in a slot in front of him. 'What's in there?' he asked.

'Oh, nothing much – open it and see.'

David pulled out some leaflets with coloured pictures, a map, and a postcard with a big plane flying over snow mountains. 'Is that Switzerland?' he asked.

'I guess so. You can write on it if you like,' said Michael. He pulled down a little shelf from the back of the seat in front of David. 'There you are, you can write on that.'

With great care David managed to print in large letters, 'LUV

TO MUM AND DAD AND SUTTY FROM DAVID.' 'I wonder if Sooty is missing me?' he thought.

Miss Green now came along with refreshments for everyone. David and Michael had a tray each, which they put on their little shelf-tables. The cup and the plate fitted into hollows in the tray – no chance to spill. There were six different kinds of sandwiches, orange squash, and a fruity ice-cream! David thought it was the loveliest meal he had ever tasted!

'Hello, Michael, who's your friend?' A tall kind-looking man in pilot's uniform was standing beside them.

'This is David, Dad. It's his first flight.'

David smiled shyly as the nice man said, "Hello, David. Enjoying yourself?'

'Dad,' said Michael eagerly, 'Could I bring him into the control cabin, just for a minute? We promise not to touch anything.'

'You'd better not!' said the pilot, leading the way through the door at the very front of the plane.

David had been wondering if the plane was flying itself while Michael's father was talking to them. Now he saw that there were two seats and a second pilot had taken over the controls. All round were look-out windows and in front of the pilots' seats were rows and rows of dials and knobs and press-buttons, 'hundreds more than in Daddy's car,' thought David. 'I'm going to be a pilot when I grow up.'

When they got back to their places, David felt quite sleepy and gave a big yawn. Michael was fiddling with the lever between their seats and laughed out loud as David, to his surprise, found himself tilting backwards. In a minute he was lying back, almost as though he were in bed. It was so comfortable and the drone of the plane made him feel so drowsy, that before he knew it he was fast asleep!

Some time later he woke with a start. The plane had given a sudden lurch. Then the pilot's voice came over the loud-speaker. 'Ladies and gentlemen, fasten your seat belts, please. We are running into an electric storm. It may be a bit choppy, but there is no cause for alarm.' So Michael was going to have his storm after all! But David felt quite safe, knowing that Michael's father and the other pilot were in charge of the plane.

Outside the sky had gone very dark and the rain was pelting down and lashing against the windows. Miss Green put the lights on and drew the boys' curtains to keep out the flashes of lightning. David thought that he could hear thunder above the noise of the engines, and felt glad that Sooty had not come with him, for he was so scared of thunder. The plane began to toss about like a bucking horse. For a minute David had an awful sick feeling. Then Michael turned and smiled at him. 'Feeling all right?' he asked. 'Fine,' answered David, knowing that he could not possibly disgrace himself before Michael.

The storm was soon over. The curtains were drawn back and David saw, far below him, the sun sparkling on peak after peak of wonderful snow mountains. They must be in Switzerland – nearly at the end of the journey! Soon the plane began to lose height and to circle round and round. Now David could see the white buildings of the airport coming into view. Very soon he would meet Aunty Vina and be able to tell her all about his wonderful adventures on his first flight.

The Airman

(Can *you* make these sounds?)

rrrrrrrrrrrrrrrrrrr

The engine roars,
The propeller spins.
'Close the doors!'
Our flight begins.

zzzzzzzzzzzzzzzz

The plane rises;
It skims the trees.
Over the houses
We fly at our ease.

mmmmmmmmmmm

zoom goes the plane,
The engine hums.
Then home again,
And down it comes. ...

mmmmmm_m_m_m
zzzzmmmmmmmmm
z
z
z
z
z
z
zzzzzzzzzrrrrrrrrrrrrrrrrrrrrrrrr

CLIVE SANSOM
From *Speech Rhymes*

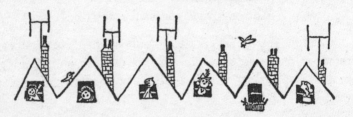

124

Johnnikin and the Fox's Tail

BY RHODA POWER

There was a fox once, and he lived in the middle of a forest, and his tail was the longest tail that ever a fox had.

There was a wee boy called Johnnikin, and he lived at the edge of the forest, and he wanted to ride on the fox's tail more than he wanted to run or skip or play.

One day his grandparents had to go into the forest to chop wood, so they made a nice bowl of soup, and they said to Johnnikin, 'Don't let anyone in while we're away, and when we come home you shall ride piggy-back.'

Johnnikin waved good-bye and shut the door, but he said, 'I don't want to ride piggy-back. I want to ride on the fox's tail.'

Well, his grandparents hadn't been gone very long before, scritch-scratch, someone came along the garden path and tapped at the door.

> 'Open, open, Johnnikin,
> Open the door and let me in.'

'I'm not allowed to!' said Johnnikin.

> 'Johnnikin, let me come inside,
> And on my tail you shall have a ride!'

When he heard that, Johnnikin jumped off his chair, opened the door, and there stood the fox, grinning. It walked straight in and, snipper-snapper-lick-a-platter, gobbled up the soup and ran away.

'Dear, dear, what did we tell you?' said Grandpapa and Grandmama when they came home and found Johnnikin crying for his dinner.

Well, next day they had to go out again, so they made a nice bowl of porridge, and said, 'Be sure you don't open the door even a crack, and when we come home you shall ride piggy-back.'

Johnnikin shut the door. 'I don't want to ride piggy-back,' he said crossly. 'I want to ride on Foxy's tail.'

He hadn't been alone very long before, scritch-scratch, someone came along the garden path and tapped at the door.

> 'Johnnikin, let me come inside,
> And on my tail you shall have a ride.'

Johnnikin crept to the door and opened it just a crack. Before he knew where he was, the fox gave it a push with his nose, walked up to the table, and snipper-snapper-lick-a-platter, gobbled up the porridge and ran away.

'What did we tell you?' said Grandpapa and Grandmama when they came home and found Johnnikin crying for his dinner. 'Dear, dear, we shall have to lock the door.'

So the next time they had to go out, Granny made a nice pot of stew, and Grandpapa locked the door and put the key in his pocket.

'Be a good boy, Johnnikin,' they said, 'and you shall ride piggy-back when we come home.'

But Johnnikin said, 'I don't want to ride piggy-back,' and he sat and kicked the legs of his chair.

He hadn't been alone for very long before he heard a polite voice say,

'Open, Johnnikin, open wide,
And on my tail you shall have a ride.'

'Go away!' shouted Johnnikin. 'You don't keep your promises and the door's locked.'

Plop! The fox jumped through the window. Snipper-snapper-lick-a-platter, it was gobbling up the stew, when, plump, down sat Johnnikin on its tail.

'Gee up!'

Out of the window jumped the fox and galloped through the forest.

'Woah!' cried Johnnikin, but the fox went faster still.

'Stop!' cried Johnnikin, but the fox went faster still. Faster, faster, faster, right into the middle of the forest and down its own hole.

And when Grandpapa and Grandmama came home, they found no dinner and no Johnnikin.

'Give me my pipe,' said Grandpapa. 'I'll play, tootle-loo, and fetch him home.'

'Give me the iron pot,' said Grandmama. 'I'll drum rub-a-dub, and fetch him home.'

And back they went into the forest till they came to the fox's hole. Then Grandpapa played on his pipe, and Grandmama drummed on her iron pot and sang a song.

'Three little foxes live within
And the fourth is Johnnikin.
We have a pipe and we have a drum,
Come and dance, little foxes, come! come! come!'

'Peep out and see who that is,' said the fox to the bigger cub.

The cub hopped out, and grandpapa caught him and shoo-ed him away out of the forest.

Then Grandpapa began to pipe and Grandmama began to drum.

'Two little foxes live within
And the third is Johnnikin.
We have a pipe and we have a drum,
Come and dance, little foxes, come! come! come!'

'Go out and see who that is and bring your brother back,' said the fox to the smaller cub.

The little cub hopped out and Grandpapa caught him and shoo-ed him away out of the forest.

Then he began to pipe and she began to drum.

'One little fox is now within,
Sitting down by Johnnikin.
We have a pipe and we have a drum,
Come and dance, little foxes, come! come! come!'

'Bother,' said the fox. 'I must go up and see for myself!'

He jumped out of the hole and 'Got you!' cried Grandpapa, and threw him into the pot and clapped on the lid.

Then Grandpapa crept down into the hole, playing his pipe very quietly.

Then Grandmama crept down after him, drumming very slowly because the pot was heavy with the fox inside it.

And they went down,
And down,
And down,
And down.
And there they found Johnnikin, crying for his Grandpapa and for Grandmama and for his dinner. So they left the fox to struggle out of the pot all by himself, and took Johnnikin home. And this time Johnnikin wanted to ride piggy-back all the way.

From *Here and There Stories*

Mustard and Cress

BY BARBARA EUPHAN TODD

Mr Martin was a market gardener, and he lived in a rather horrid little seaside town where the sand was grey instead of being golden and where there were no rocky pools. This did not worry Mr Martin at all. He was busy and happy enough because he had green fingers, as had his father and his grandfather before him.

As everyone knows, people with green fingers can make almost anything grow, and people with green thumbs can make *everything* grow. Mr Martin's thumbs were as bright as grass on a Spring morning, and a little brighter than his eight fingers. Nobody in the town of Flatsea knew about this because, like all gardeners, he liked his hands to be earthy. He seldom washed them until after dusk, and he kept a pair of leather gauntlets handy for popping on.

On Sunday mornings, when he went to church, he wore brown kid gloves, and Fred, his grandson, wore grey woollen ones unless it was too hot, when he was allowed to wear a clean thumb-stall instead. There was a reason for this. The top joint of the little boy's left thumb was as green as grass, and he was left-handed.

Fred had not worn a thumb-stall all his life. When he was too little to know better, he was fond of sucking his left thumb. It kept it clean and it kept it out of sight and out of danger.

Before Fred was big enough to go to school, Mr Martin taught him to write his name on the sand. They printed it in pebbles that were all of the same size and in bits of driftwood

that were not the same size, and in shells, that were as near the same size as Fred could find, and in strands of seaweed that were as flat as hair-ribbons.

One day, they wrote it in donkey hooves!

There was a dear little seaside donkey whose name was Nero. His ears were long and grey, and their linings were as soft as thistledown. He belonged to Mr Sprott who let out deck-chairs at twopence for a short sit and threepence for a longer sit, and sixpence for an all-day sit.

It was Nero's job to give donkey rides to visitors at twopence for a short ride and fourpence for a longer ride and sixpence for the longest ride to the pier and back. Nero did not enjoy his work (unless the rides were very short sits indeed) because some of the riders were too heavy for him, and most of them lumped about on his back, and made it sore. He was fond of Fred because the boy did not weigh much more than a net full of shrimps.

So, when Mr Martin said, 'Up you get, boy. We'll write your

131

name in donkey-hooves,' Nero did not mind a bit. He pricked up his ears and laughed – 'He-haw! He-haw! Hee-hee!'

Mr Sprott did not mind either because he was sitting in one of his own deck-chairs, and reading a newspaper.

'How can I write my name in donkey-hooves?' asked Fred.

'You'll see,' said Mr Martin. 'Up you get.'

The tide had gone out, and the beach was quite empty except for some seagulls who made mewing noises as Fred put his feet into the stirrups.

'Here we go!' said Mr Martin, taking hold of Nero's bridle, and leading him towards the sea, 'Gently does it.'

He led the donkey in a straight line to the water's edge, and then in a straight line along the edge. Then back-along and down-along and out-along, and back-along-and-down.

'Now look!' said Mr Martin, and he turned Nero's soft nose towards the sea again.

Fred looked, and there in donkey hoof marks was the first letter of his own first name – F. He sat up straight because he felt so proud and grand. That first letter was as long as the breakwater.

'Gently does it,' said Mr Martin, leading Nero towards the sea.

By tea-time, the whole of the name – FRED MARTIN – was written over the length and breadth in donkey hoof marks, and Nero was stamping the full stop at the end.

'Now look again,' said Mr Martin.

'It's so big!' gasped Fred, after he had looked and looked again. 'Tell you what. It's as big as anything. I wrote it myself.'

'You wrote it and I wrote it and Nero wrote it,' said Mr Martin. 'And if you're big enough to write your own name in big letters, you should be big enough to stop sucking your thumb.'

Now that is where Mr Martin made a big mistake. Fred took his thumb out of his mouth, and stroked Nero's nose, and put his left hand into his left hand pocket, and thought to himself, 'I am too big to suck my thumb.'

At tea-time he held his cup in his left hand, and with his right hand he picked up the buttered toast that was spread with crab-apple jelly which tasted so much better than his own green thumb.

After tea he ran to the end of the garden, and looked down to the beach because he wanted to see the big letters of his own name. He should have remembered that the tide would treat them as it had treated the sticks and pebbles and seaweed that had spelled the words – FRED MARTIN – but he had been too excited to think of anything unhappy. So there he stood, looking down at the sulky grey water that had almost covered the beach and quite covered the donkey's hoof marks.

He knew that if he was too big to suck his thumb he was too big to cry either, so he sniffed sadly. Mr Martin, who had followed him out of the bungalow, heard the sniffs, and guessed what had happened.

'Never you mind,' said he. 'I'll show you how to write your name in mustard and cress. There's a seed bed all ready for sowing. You come along with me.'

'Seeds take so long to grow,' sniffed Fred.

'These ones are quick growers,' said Mr Martin, and he took a packet of mustard and cress from his waistcoat pocket. Then he picked up a stick that was lying handy, and wrote the name, FRED MARTIN on the soft brown earth.

'Those letters are a lot smaller than the letters on the beach,' sniffed Fred.

Mr Martin did not answer. He opened the packets, and let the seeds trickle quite thickly into the writing on the earth. When he had finished he covered them up.

'You can't see anything now,' sniffed Fred.

'You will when you've run three times round the apple-tree at the bottom of the garden,' said his grandfather. He slipped off his leather gauntlets, and with his green fingers and greener thumbs he stroked the earth above the seeds.

When Fred came back, rather out of puff, but in a very much better temper, there was his name in green letters that stretched from end to end of the seed bed, and the mustard and cress that spelled it was just the right height for cutting.

'Write *your* name now,' begged Fred.

'No!' Mr Martin shook his head. 'It's best to be mean with magic, or else it goes wrong.'

'Why?' asked Fred.

'Because you can have too much of a good thing. If you lived in a sweet shop, you wouldn't be fond of sweets for very long.'

Fred thought about bull's-eyes and toffee and butterscotch, and chocolate and peppermint creams until he felt hungry. Then he thought of mixed fruitdrops and sugar mice and caramels until he stopped feeling hungry.

'You see,' went on Mr Martin, just as though the thoughts had been spoken out aloud. 'You see the day would come when you would rather have mustard and cress sandwiches for supper.'

He put the rest of the seeds away in the potting shed while Fred went to find the scissors.

They *had* mustard-and-cress sandwiches for supper, but the name – FRED MARTIN – still stretched across the garden bed. It was written in little white stems, as fine as hairs. When the moon came up, they shone like silver.

Next morning, Mr Martin was busy, and Fred's left thumb itched and twitched in his pocket because it had been so used to being in his mouth.

The packets, that were still half-full of mustard-and-cress seed, lay on the potting-shed shelf.

'Tell you what,' said Fred to himself. "Tell you what, I'll write my name in the market square.'

He picked up the packets, and he picked up a stick, and he ran into the town. The market square was empty, except for a coach. The coach was empty, too. Half an hour before it had been filled with children, their Sunday School teachers, and one very old grandmother, who had all been driven to Flatsea for a treat. Fred did not know this. All he knew was that the dust lay thickly round the coach, that he had a stick and some packets of seeds, and that his left thumb was itching and twitching like Billy-o.

135

The stick, helped by his right hand, made wobbly letters in the dust all round the coach. Then, Fred took a pinch of seed between his left forefinger and his green thumb, and began to sow them in the marks he had made with the stick. When he had finished, he straightened his back.

'Tell you what,' he said to himself. 'Tell you what, I'll run three times round the lamp post, and then I'll LOOK.'

Round and round and round he ran, and then he LOOKED. Yes, the mustard and cress had come up nicely, and it was quite ready for cutting. The name – FRED MARTIN – was written in green straggly letters all round the coach. It was a pity there was no one there to see them except a seagull that had come to perch on top of the market hall.

'Tell you what,' said Fred to himself. 'Tell you what. I won't cut it till just before tea. Then we'll have mustard-and-cress sandwiches again.'

That afternoon, Mr Martin set him to work wheeling sand to the potting-shed. To and fro went Fred with his little barrow.

'That will give you a good appetite for tea,' said Mr Martin. 'But before we have it, I want you to run down to the market square, and tell Mr Jones at the sweet shop that his plants are ready for him. He can pick them up this evening.'

Fred tipped up his barrow, and rushed into the bungalow.

'Hi!' shouted Mr Martin. 'That's not the way to the market square.' But Fred did not hear him. He had snatched up the scissors from their place on the dresser, and was picking up a basket.

He ran full tilt into the town. This time the square was full of people. The firemen were there, and so was the policeman. So were Mr Jones from the sweet shop and Mrs Brown from

the newspaper shop, the driver of the coach, the school children, the teachers, and the very old grandmother.

'Tell you what,' said Fred to himself. 'They are all looking at my name.'

They WERE all looking at his name and the name had grown so high and so strongly that the curly leaves of the cress and the round leaves of the mustard were joined together in a thick green mat over the roof of the coach. They were as big as rhubarb leaves, and a fireman was standing waist-deep in the middle of them, As for the stems, they were as tough as bamboos.

'It's a jungle, that's what it is,' said the very old grandmother. 'The driver shouldn't have driven into a jungle.'

'Someone must have moved the coach,' said the driver sulkily. 'I've been driving for twenty years, and never had an accident.'

'Well you've had one now,' shrieked the very old grandmother. 'You've had one now, young man, and no mistake. Let me tell you, I left my knitting on the front seat. What are

you going to do about that when my grandchildren need their warm socks for the winter? How will you feel when they have to go barefoot except for chilblains?'

The driver did not answer. Fred took his left hand out of his pocket and stared at his green thumb, and felt, sadly, that everything was his fault.

'Please, Mr Jones,' he whispered. 'Please, Mr Jones, Grandfather says –' But Mr Jones was too busy sawing at a cress stem to hear the whisper.

A couple of firemen were blunting their axes on the mustard stems.

All the little boys clattered their tin spades, and sang:

> 'We won't go home till morning!
> We won't go home till morning!'

Some little girls joined hands, and danced round the lamp-post.

'We'd better set fire to the stuff,' said Mrs Brown from the newspaper shop. 'We'd better burn it down.'

'I sell good fire-lighters at sixpence a bundle!' shouted Mr Carter, the ironmonger, and he hurried into his shop to fetch them.

'If you set fire to all that stuff, you'll set fire to the coach,' said the driver. 'The tank's full of petrol.'

'Don't dare to set fire to my knitting!' yelled the very old grandmother. 'If you set fire to my knitting, I'll have the law on you.'

The policeman, who had been writing things in his notebook, looked up, and said, 'If a fire BREAKS out, it is the duty of the fire brigade to PUT it out.'

'Help! Help!' cried a muffled voice from the top of the coach, as the third fireman, who was helmet-high now in mustard and cress, tried to make himself heard.

'We need the steeplejack,' said the policeman, 'or we shall need him soon.'

'The steeplejack's away on the bell-ringers' outing,' said Mrs Brown. 'I know that because I saw his aunt only yesterday.'

'Help! Help!' whimpered the fireman on top of the coach.

'Weed-killer, that's what we want,' screamed the very old grandmother. 'Weed-killer or Jungle-killer. I don't mind which you use as long as you use it quickly, and save my knitting.'

Just then, Mr Martin walked into the market square. He was carrying a box of bedding plants for Mr Jones, because he wanted to save the sweet-shop man the trouble of walking up the hill.

First he looked at Fred, who was looking sadly at his own green thumb, and then he looked at the very old grandmother, who was shrieking, 'Weed-killer! Weed-killer! Weed-killer!'

'No,' said Mr Martin slowly. 'No, you don't want weed-killer, you want mustard-and-cress killer. Eh, Fred?'

Fred put his green thumb and the whole of his left hand into his pocket.

'Do you call that stuff mustard and cress?' yelled the very old grandmother.

'I call it what it is,' answered Mr Martin. 'Eh, Fred?' Then he slipped off his right-hand leather gauntlet, and fumbled in his waistcoat pocket, and brought out a pinch of something that looked like dust and smelled like pepper. Indeed it smelled and worked so very much like pepper that all the people began to sneeze until their eyes were filled with tears. Because of that, they did not see Mr Martin's green fingers and thumbs, as he sprinkled the dust all round the coach.

At once, the leaves of the mustard and cress began to curl up and dwindle.

'Whew!' whistled the fireman on top of the coach, as the mustard-and-cress leaves shrank down to his middle. 'Whew! That was a near thing.'

> 'We won't go home till morning!
> We won't go home till morning!'

shouted the little boys, as they clattered their tin spades.

'Maybe you won't,' said Mr Martin, and he glanced at the little girls who were dancing round the lamp post, as happily as though they were jigging round a maypole. 'Maybe you won't, but Granny shall go back to her knitting.'

He put one last dollop of mustard-and-cress killer at the foot of the coach steps.

At once, the stems of the mustard and cress died down, so that the very old grandmother and the teachers and the driver could climb into the coach.

'I'm sorry,' said Mr Martin. 'I'm sorry, but I haven't enough mustard-and-cress killer left to make a good clean job of it. So –'

'*We won't go home till morning,*' said the little boys.

'That's just about it,' agreed Mr Martin. 'Come along, Fred.' Then while the very old grandmother picked up her knitting and the third fireman shook a cress leaf from his helmet, and the children ran back to the beach, Fred followed his grand-father up to the bungalow.

'I shall have to make you a thumb-stall,' said Mr Martin. 'And you will have to wear it until you have learned to be mean with magic. There's no two ways about it.'

From *The Boy with the Green Thumb*

Seven at One Blow

TRADITIONAL

Once upon a time, a tailor sat sewing. At his side was a plate with a piece of bread and jam upon it. It was a hot day and flies were buzzing everywhere, especially round the jam because it was so sweet.

'Botheration take them!' cried the little tailor and he brought down his pressing-cloth on top of them. When he lifted it, there lay seven dead flies with their legs in the air.

'Seven at one blow!' exclaimed the tailor. 'What a hero I am!' and he made himself a belt and wrote on it, SEVEN AT ONE BLOW. 'I must go out into the world,' he said. 'Such a man as I am cannot stay in this small town.' So he set out at once, taking with him a piece of cheese in his pocket and a pet bird on his wrist and singing as he went.

Before long he met a giant as tall as the tallest tree. 'How would you like to come with me on my travels?' he shouted up to the giant. 'Do you see how strong I am – I have just killed seven at one blow.'

'We shall soon see who is the stronger,' said the giant, scornfully. 'Can you do this?' and he picked up a stone and squeezed it so hard that water dripped from it.

'That's nothing!' boasted the little tailor and he took the cheese from his pocket and squeezed it until the whey ran out like a river.

'Hm-m,' grunted the giant. 'Try this,' and he threw a stone high up in the air, higher than the clouds.

'Your stone came back again – mine will go so high that we

shall never see it again,' shouted the little tailor and he threw his bird into the air. Naturally when the bird found itself free, it flew away and did not return.

'Hm-m,' grumbled the giant, rather surprised. 'Let's see how you can work. We'll carry this tree together.' And he lifted a fallen tree as long as from here to there.

'I'll take the heaviest end where the branches are,' said the tailor and he skipped into the leaves where he could not be seen, so that the giant, without knowing it, carried tree and tailor as well. Presently he was so tired that he dropped the tree with a groan.

Out hopped the tailor. 'Are you tired so soon?' he asked in great surprise. 'I'm as fresh as a daisy!' and he sang and whistled as they went along together.

In the forest was a wild apple tree. The giant reached up and pulled down a branch and picked some apples. 'You are welcome to help yourself,' he said to the tailor. 'Catch!' and he let the branch go.

The little tailor could not hold the branch at all and was

flung into the air and came down with a bump that nearly knocked out his teeth.

'Couldn't you hold down that little twig?' said the giant scornfully.

'Hold it down! I was jumping over the top of the tree – didn't you see that huntsman just about to shoot? I only just got out of the way in time,' said the little tailor.

The giant was very angry indeed. He invited the little man to spend the night with him. 'I'll soon get rid of this grass-hopper,' he thought.

The tailor went with him to a great cave where several giants sat, eating a whole sheep with their fingers. Then he was given a bed as large as a room. Directly he was alone, the tailor put the pillow in a corner and lay down on that, for it was quite big enough for him.

In the middle of the night, the giant came and whacked the

bed with a great stick. 'That's finished off that "Seven at one blow" creature,' he said, and went back to bed.

In the morning when the giants had gone out, the little tailor came out from his hiding-place and set off on his travels again, whistling as he went. On the road he met the soldiers of the King and when they saw that he had killed 'Seven at one blow', they told their master that here was a mighty fighter who would be very useful. So the King gave him a fine house in which to live.

One day the King said: 'If you'll go and get rid of two great giants who are robbing and killing my people, I'll let you marry my daughter and give you half my kingdom as well.'

'Oh, all right,' said the little tailor. 'What are two to a man who has killed seven at one blow!'

At last he found the giants. They were asleep under a tree and snoring so hard that each breath caused a storm in the trees overhead. The little tailor filled a bag with stones and climbed up into a tree.

Presently he threw a stone and hit the first giant on the nose. At once he awoke and roared at his brother: 'What do you mean by hitting me on the nose! How dare you!'

'I didn't,' answered the second giant and, after quarrelling for a while, they fell asleep again.

The little tailor threw another stone, and this time he hit the second giant on the nose. Immediately he sprang up and punched the first giant. 'Now it's my turn!' he roared.

They began to fight and thump each other for all they were worth. The little tailor was nearly shaken out of his tree, but the end of it was that the giants killed each other.

But when the little tailor told the King what he had done, he refused to give him his reward. 'I've another task for you to do,'

he said. 'You must catch the unicorn which is running wild in the forest and bring it back alive.'

'What is one unicorn to me!' said the tailor, waving his sword. 'I could catch seven.'

He went off to the forest, taking with him an axe and a coil of rope. Here came the unicorn rushing through the forest, its one horn sticking out of its forehead like a spear.

The tailor stood bravely in its path until the very last moment, then – hey presto! – he skipped out of the way and the unicorn's horn stuck fast in the tree.

Out jumped the little tailor, put a rope round the unicorn's neck and then chopped part of the trunk away so that the beast could pull out its horn. Very cross it was too, but what could it do?

Still the little tailor was refused his just reward. 'I have one last task for you,' said the King. 'Catch the wild boar that is killing my woodcutters in the forest.'

'What is one wild boar!' boasted the tailor. 'Seven at one blow is my motto.'

He went into the forest, whistling and singing, and there was the wild boar and what terrible large tusks it had!

The tailor ran for his life, while the boar thundered after him. Suddenly the little man skipped in at the door of an old cottage. In rushed the boar after him. With a hop and a jump, the tailor leapt out of the window, rushed round the cottage and shut the door. The boar was a prisoner and very angry he was too, but what could he do about it?

So now the King could refuse the tailor his reward no longer and he married the King's daughter. When the King died, the little tailor became King in his place and a very good King he was.

And all because he had killed seven flies at one blow!

Marmaduke is in a Jam

BY ELIZABETH CHAPMAN

Marmaduke, the little red lorry, and Joe, his driver, were in London. It was their first morning there, and they were very excited as they drove through the busy streets. There was no time for singing their song, and no time for talking, for Marmaduke had never seen so many cars and buses and lorries, and he had to be very careful how he went along.

'I mustn't get into any trouble here,' he said to himself. 'I don't want all these people to think we don't know how to drive down in Yorkshire, but it really is much more difficult here than driving across the hills at home. It's noisy too. I don't think my friend, Horace the hill-sheep, would be very happy here.'

Marmaduke and Joe drove very well indeed, and were very pleased when bus drivers waved them on, just as though they were real Londoners, and were even more pleased when, after Marmaduke had done a very difficult turn to the right across a line of cars, a lorry driver leaned out of his cab and called:

'That's what I call good driving. Keep it up, mate.'

'We'll go and look at the River Thames first,' said Joe, and on they drove, feeling happy and proud.

After a while they came to the river. They halted for a while to look at Big Ben and the Houses of Parliament. Then they drove slowly along the Embankment, looking at all the buildings and the boats and the long, graceful bridges over the broad river.

Just past one of the bridges they stopped to admire an old

sailing-ship with very high masts. The ship was so old that she didn't go to sea any more, but in days gone by she had seen many foreign lands.

'What a grand old ship she is,' Marmaduke said, and then he nearly jumped out of his red paint.

For, suddenly, the decks of the ship were full of boys in Sea Scout uniforms, all hanging over the rails and waving and shouting.

'Hello, Marmaduke! Hello, Joe!' they called. 'Good old Marmaduke! Come to see us, have you?'

'Well, I don't know!' smiled Marmaduke. 'They're *our* Sea Scouts, Joe. You know, the Sea Scouts from home. We once helped them with a jumble sale and I got sold by mistake. Do you remember?'

'Why, so they are,' said Joe. 'Well, I never!'

The boys ran down the gangway from the ship, and were soon chatting away like anything to the two friends, telling them that they were spending a holiday on the ship.

'We're going to see the Changing of the Guard at Buckingham Palace,' said Marmaduke presently.

'Oh, I wish we could see that,' said one of the boys.

'Well, ask the officer in charge of you if you can come with us,' said Joe.

So off they ran, and soon they were back all smiles, so that Marmaduke and Joe knew that the officer had said yes.

They all climbed into the back of the lorry with their sailor hats perched very correct and straight on their heads, and away they went to Buckingham Palace.

What a merry drive it was! Several people turned round to smile and wave at the bright red lorry with its load of cheering sailor-boys.

Then they turned into a very busy street and ... stopped!

One of the boys put his head round the corner of the lorry into the cab.

'What's the matter?' he asked Joe. 'Not broken down, have you? Not Marmaduke?'

'Of course not,' said Marmaduke, a little bit put out that any-one should think he would break down for no reason at all. 'I just can't get through, that's all. There are so many cars and buses, we're all in a jam, and can't move.'

'Well, it isn't the kind of jam I like,' said the Sea Scout. 'I like strawberries in mine.'

The boys giggled, the cars and buses moved on, and Marma-duke moved, too. Then they stopped and Marmaduke stopped, too.

A motor-cyclist rode up beside Marmaduke.

'Excuse me,' said Joe to the motor-cyclist. 'Does this happen often, and how long do you think we'll be?'

'It happens every day somewhere in London,' replied the motor-cyclist. 'And you'll probably be here for ages. Why, are you going somewhere in a hurry?'

'We're going to see the Changing of the Guard at Bucking-ham Palace,' said Joe.

'You'll miss that at this rate,' said the motor-cyclist.

Marmaduke and Joe and the Sea Scouts waited gloomily.

'We're going home tomorrow,' said one of the boys, 'so we won't see it after all.'

'We're off now,' sang out Marmaduke.

Sure enough, the cars and buses were moving, and Marmaduke and Joe and the Sea Scouts looked cheerful again, but not for long. Soon they stopped once more.

'Oh dear!' said Marmaduke, and sighed heavily.

The motor-cyclist started up his engine.

'Here, follow me!' he said. 'Down that street there.'

Marmaduke had halted beside a little side street to the left of him, and very quickly Joe turned him into the street, and they were soon following the motor-cyclist. It was quiet down this

street, and the motor-cyclist led them through one little street after another, round corners, up and down little hills, until Marmaduke was once more feeling a little dizzy.

And then suddenly they were riding down the tree-lined road to Buckingham Palace.

'I'll leave you here,' called the motor-cyclist. 'Hope you enjoy it.' And with his engine throbbing merrily, away he darted before Marmaduke or Joe or any of the boys had time to say thank you.

'That *was* kind of him,' said Marmaduke. 'Now we shall be in time.'

When they reached the Palace, a very helpful policeman told Marmaduke where he could stand, and soon through the Palace gates came the soldiers, the band leading them playing a stirring march.

How smart they looked with the sun shining on their bright red uniforms, and their black fur bearskins, and how straight they marched. As they passed Marmaduke and Joe, all the Sea Scouts stood to attention in the back of the lorry and saluted, and got a special cheer from the crowd. An American gentleman came and took a photograph of them. He asked Joe for his name and address so that he could send them one.

Too soon it was over, and Marmaduke and Joe took the boys back to their ship. There were no jams this time. When the boys were back on the ship, they again stood to attention and saluted as Marmaduke and Joe, the sun shining on their red paint and black tyres, drove smartly away.

From *Marmaduke and the Lambs*

The Donkey

I saw a donkey
  One day old,
His head was too big
  For his neck to hold;
His legs were shaky,
  And long, and loose,
They rocked and staggered
  And weren't much use.
He tried to gambol
  And frisk a bit,
But he wasn't quite sure
  Of the trick of it.
His queer little coat
  Was soft and grey
And curled at his neck
  In a lovely way.
His face was wistful
  And left no doubt
That he felt life needed
  Some thinking out.
So he blundered round
  In venturous quest,
And then lay flat
  On the ground to rest.

He looked so little,
  And weak and slim,
I prayed the world
  Might be good to him.

GERTRUDE HINDE

Why the Robin Has a Red Breast

TRADITIONAL

Once upon a time, in the cold lands of the north where there is snow and ice all winter long, there lived a man with his little son. It was so cold that they wore clothes of fur and their home was a hut made of hard snow.

But, although they were so warmly dressed, they needed a fire as well. With a fire they could have hot food and dry their wet clothes and be really warm. They kept it alight all the time at the entrance to their hut, and never left it without someone to watch it. If the father went out hunting, the son stayed by the fire, feeding it with twigs. If the boy slept, his father tended it. It was the most precious thing they had.

Now the great white bear who lived in those parts hated the man and his son because they hunted him. The bear thought that if the fire went out, so that they were without warmth, they would fall asleep and grow so cold that they woke no more. If he could only get rid of them, there would be no one to hunt him, for these two were the only people in that part of the north.

Often the bear watched the fire, hoping that he might be able to destroy it, but the man or his son was always there and the bear dared not go too near.

One day the father fell ill and lay all day on his bed of furs in the hut. His little son looked after him as well as he could, but he dared not go hunting and he dared not let the fire go out. There was little to eat in the hut, and hour by hour the boy grew more tired and sleepy. At night he could hear the great white bear snuffling and padding round the hut, and he knew that if the fire went out there would be nothing to protect him.

At last the time came when the boy could stay awake no longer. His eyes closed, his head nodded, and he fell into a deep sleep.

Then the great white bear crept past the sleeping boy and trampled out the tiny fire with his big, wet paws, until only grey ash remained. Away he padded across the snow, feeling sure that the man and his son would soon trouble him no more.

The boy slept, his father tossed in fever, and it grew colder and colder round the hut. Icicles hung from the trees and all was still. The boy and his father were stiff from cold. The bear watched from a distance.

Now the boy had a friend, a small, brown bird, a robin. Whenever he had any food, the boy would feed his little friend.

The robin came hopping and fluttering round the hut, but no one came to give it food and the bright, warm thing that people call fire was dull and grey.

'Wake up, wake up!' it cried to the boy. 'It is cold – the fire is out!'

But the boy slept on.

'Cheep-cheep!' cried the robin again. 'Wake up!' It scratched amongst the ashes to find a little warmth, and there was a tiny spark of fire. 'Cheep-cheep!' it cried once more, and began to fan the spark with its wings.

But the boy slept on.

As the little bird fluttered its wings, a tiny flame sprang up and spread an inch or two. The robin worked harder than ever until its feathers were quite scorched with the heat.

'Cheep-cheep!' it cried again. More twigs caught alight and the fire grew brighter, but the little robin felt that soon its own feathers would burst into flames, they were so hot! It was so tired that it could go on no longer.

But the air was warm. The boy was awake. 'The fire!' he exclaimed. 'Oh, the fire!' He jumped up and threw the last twigs on to the flames so that they blazed up.

'I am quite well again, my son,' said a voice behind him, and there was his father, quite recovered from his illness. As he came forward to warm his hands over the fire, a little brown bird flew away. 'Cheep-cheep!' it cried – but the man and the boy did not hear its tiny voice.

And they never knew why the robin had a red breast from that day onwards, or that they owed their lives to a little brown bird.

Midsummer Day

BY MARGARET GORE

It all began in a field. In one corner was a little hut, rather old and shabby; in another corner lay two wheels and an old chimney-pot and a pile of rusty nails. Sometimes they had a little grumble amongst themselves.

'Oh dear, what's the use of lying here day after day. I wish I could run again,' one of the wheels would say.

'I feel very useless, too,' said the chimney-pot.

And the little hut who could hear what they were saying would agree: 'What use are we – and it's so dull!'

But on Midsummer's Day – which is a magic time – something very exciting happened. First of all there was a thunderstorm, with a lot of lightning that came zigzagging across the sky and plenty of big claps of thunder. Then suddenly all sorts of queer things began to happen. The two big wheels got up and ran across the field towards the little hut. At the same time, all the old nails began jumping up and down and then started leap-frogging across the field.

Before you could say 'knife', the two wheels joined themselves on to the little hut and the nails drove themselves in to make them secure. Along came the old chimney-pot and hopped on to the roof.

'My, my!' said the little hut. 'Whatever is happening to me? I can move, I can run. I've got two lovely big wheels. Come on, let's go for a spin.'

By now the thunder and lightning had died down and the sun was shining. So off went the little hut, across the field,

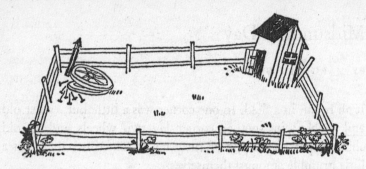

through the open gate, and down the hill, down, down, down. At last he came to a halt on a patch of grass beside the road. He was puffing a bit for he had never run like that in his life before.

He yawned and shut his window eye and was just dozing off in the warm sunshine when there came a small tap-tapping at the door.

'Goodness, what's that! Who's there!'

'It's me. I'm Mollie,' a voice answered.

'Come in, come in,' said the little hut. 'Just push the door open.'

The door wasn't easy to open for it had been shut for such a long time, but at last it burst open with a jerk and in came a little girl.

'Sit down and make yourself at home,' said the little hut kindly. 'I think I have a chair somewhere – and a table too.'

'So you have,' said the little girl, sitting down comfortably. 'How cosy it is here.'

'Stay as long as you like,' said the little hut. 'It will be nice to have company.'

'Thank you. What's your name?' asked Mollie.

158

'I don't really know – at least I've forgotten. I think it's written over my door. Could you have a look, please?'

Mollie ran outside to look. Sure enough there were some letters over the door, but they were very faint. 'The first letter is s,' she called, 'then there are two letters I can't read, then an H, then an E farther on and the last letter is N. SHEN – that's a nice name!'

'SHEN will do very nicely,' said the little hut contentedly.

Mollie picked some buttercups in the field and some honeysuckle from the hedge and put them in a glass jar on the table. They looked very pretty there and the little hut was pleased.

'Where are you going to sleep tonight?' worried Shen. 'I don't think I have a bed.'

'There's plenty of hay in the field,' said Mollie. She fetched armfuls of hay and made herself a hay pillow with her red scarf over it, a hay mattress, and a warm hay eiderdown to cover her.

'Good night, dear Shen,' she said drowsily and in a few

moments she was fast asleep, and Shen closed his window-eye and slept too.

The sun was shining when Shen and Mollie woke next morning and a little donkey was looking in at the door.

'Hee-haw,' brayed the little donkey. 'Where are you off to?'

'Nowhere,' said Shen.

'Oh, dear Shen, couldn't we go somewhere? It would be such fun,' begged Mollie.

'Why not?' agreed Shen. 'Let's go for a spin,' and he was just about to set off when he noticed that the donkey was looking sad and lonely.

'Would you like to come with us?' asked the little hut. 'You could trot behind.'

'Oh, thank you,' said the little donkey. 'My name is Jeremy.'

'It's odd,' said Shen, 'but I've a feeling in my floorboards there is somewhere I want to go, but I can't quite remember where.'

Away rolled the little hut with Mollie looking out of the window and Jeremy trotting behind. How lovely it was to be moving! The trees and the houses seemed to hurry past as they ran down and down and down, through a village and up the hill on the other side.

Suddenly Shen pulled up so sharply that poor Jeremy bumped his nose. A brown field-mouse was sitting right in the middle of the road.

'Now, now,' said Shen, 'you mustn't sit there, you know. I might have run over you.'

'I'm sorry,' squeaked the mouse, 'but I thought someone might give me a lift. I'm so tired of walking.'

'You poor little thing!' exclaimed Mollie, jumping out. 'Of course you can have a ride. Come and sit on the hay with me.'

In jumped the mouse, away rolled Shen, while Mollie and Jeremy listened to the mouse's story. He told them that his name was Lucky Dip because he had been born in a bran-tub, but the tub had been emptied and he had to run away to find a new home. Soon Lucky Dip was fast asleep in the hay while Shen rolled on gaily, Mollie looked out of the window, and Jeremy trotted behind.

That night the friends camped under a big oak tree. They were just settling down to sleep when they heard several small explosions overhead.

'Good gracious!' said Shen. 'Something's sitting on my head.'

'Can you see anything, Jeremy?' called Mollie.

'I can see a dark shape. What can it be?'

'Shall I run up on Shen's head and see what it is?' squeaked Lucky Dip.

'Be careful, Lucky Dip,' said Mollie. 'It – whatever it is – might bite.'

Lucky Dip, feeling very brave, puffed out his chest and ran on to Shen's roof. Just at that moment a lorry rattled by and, in the light of its headlamps, Lucky Dip saw a squirrel cracking nuts busily. 'It's only a squirrel,' he called and everyone ran out to look.

'Well, what are you all staring at, if I may ask? Haven't you seen a squirrel before?' asked the squirrel.

'I'm so sorry,' said Shen. 'Why don't you come inside and finish your supper. Your nut-shells are tickling my head.'

By the time the squirrel had finished his supper, they were all good friends. He told them that his name was Pickpocket because he was rather good at taking nuts out of people's pockets without their knowing.

'That's a *bad* thing to do,' said Mollie.

'I only do it for fun,' explained Pickpocket. 'I give the nuts back afterwards.'

He was such a jolly little fellow that they were all pleased when he asked if he could go with them on their journey.

Next morning off they went again with Pickpocket perched on the table, Lucky Dip on his bed of hay, Mollie at the window looking out, and Jeremy trotting behind.

'We're getting quite a large family,' said Mollie. 'I wonder if anyone else will join us.'

As it happened, someone else did join them, but in a rather unexpected way. After dinner, they heard a weak cry which seemed to come from the bushes near by. Mollie ran across to look, followed by Lucky Dip and Pickpocket.

There on the ground lay a wounded seagull. He had hurt himself on some barbed wire. Mollie carried him back to the hut and bathed his cuts carefully. 'I must get back!' the seagull said over and over again.

'Where do you want to go?' asked Mollie. But the poor seagull was too weak to tell her.

'He'd better come with us,' said Shen. 'And let's go quickly. I feel in my floorboards that we are near the end of our journey.'

Away he ran at top speed – Jeremy had to trot quite fast to keep up – while the others looked after the seagull.

'We're nearly there!' cried Shen.

'Nearly where?' asked everyone.

'Look!' Up the road came a family – father, mother, and two children. Each of the children carried a bucket and spade.

'Buckets and spades! That reminds me of something – but I can't stop to think now,' shouted Shen excitedly.

The little hut was puffing and panting, he was running so fast, but at last the road came to an end – and there was the SEA!

'This is where I belong!' cried Shen as he ran on to the sands.

'This is where *I* belong too – I feel better already!' cried the seagull. 'Thank you, dear friends – I'll come and see you soon, but I must go home.' Away he flew high, high into the sky until they could see him no longer.

'Let's go for a paddle!' cried Shen.

But when he tried to run, his wheels stuck fast in the sand and he could not move an inch. The tide was coming in fast

and very soon a big wave came up and washed over his little steps. And he liked it!

Suddenly Shen remembered everything! He remembered being by the sea when he was young, and children laughing and playing on the sands, and the ice-cream man and the Punch and Judy show and the donkeys and the seagulls.

'Mollie, Mollie,' he cried. 'I've remembered my name. It's SEAHAVEN and I'm a beach hut!'

So Mollie painted Shen's name over his door in fine red paint, and each day she played on the sands with Jeremy, Lucky Dip, and Pickpocket.

But Shen stood in the warm sand with the sea lapping over his toes and wheels and looked out over the sea. How happy he was to be home again!

The Little Rooster and the Diamond Button

BY KATE SEREDY

Somewhere, at some place beyond the Seven Seas, there lived a poor old woman. The poor old woman had a Little Rooster. One day the Little Rooster walked out of the yard to look for strange insects and worms. All the insects and worms in the yard were his friends – he was hungry, but he could not eat his friends! So he walked out to the road. He scratched and he scratched. He scratched out a Diamond Button. Of all things, a Diamond Button! The Button twinkled at him. 'Pick me up, Little Rooster, and take me to your old mistress. She likes Diamond Buttons.'

'Cock-a-doodle-doo. I'll pick you up and take you to my poor old mistress!'

So he picked up the Button. Just then the Turkish Sultan walked by. The Turkish Sultan was very, very fat. Three fat servants walked behind him, carrying the wide, wide bag of the Turkish Sultan's trousers. He saw the Little Rooster with the Diamond Button.

'Little Rooster, give me your Diamond Button.'

'No, indeed, I won't. I am going to give it to my poor old mistress. She likes Diamond Buttons.'

But the Turkish Sultan liked Diamond Buttons, too. Besides, he could not take 'no' for an answer. He turned to his three fat servants.

'Catch the Little Rooster and take the Diamond Button from him.'

The three fat servants dropped the wide, wide bag of the Turkish Sultan's trousers, caught the Little Rooster, and took the Diamond Button away from him. The Turkish Sultan took the Diamond Button home with him and put it in his treasure chamber.

The Little Rooster was very angry. He went to the palace of the Turkish Sultan, perched on the window, and cried:

'Cock-a-doodle-doo! Turkish Sultan, give me back my Diamond Button.'

The Turkish Sultan did not like this, so he walked into another room.

The Little Rooster perched on the window of another room and cried: 'Cock-a-doodle-doo! Turkish Sultan, give me back my Diamond Button.'

The Turkish Sultan was mad. He called his three fat servants.

'Catch the Little Rooster. Throw him into the well, let him drown!'

The three fat servants caught the Little Rooster and threw him into the well. But the Little Rooster cried: 'Come, my empty stomach, come, my empty stomach, drink up all the water.'

His empty stomach drank up all the water.

The Little Rooster flew back to the window and cried: 'Cock-a-doodle-doo! Turkish Sultan, give me back my Diamond Button.'

The Turkish Sultan was madder than before. He called his three fat servants.

'Catch the Little Rooster and throw him into the fire. Let him burn!'

The three fat servants caught the Little Rooster and threw him into the fire.

But the Little Rooster cried: 'Come, my full stomach, let out all the water to put out all the fire.'

His full stomach let out all the water. It put out all the fire.

He flew back to the window again and cried: 'Cock-a-doodle-doo! Turkish Sultan, give me back my Diamond Button.'

The Turkish Sultan was madder than ever. He called his three fat servants.

'Catch the Little Rooster, throw him into a beehive, and let the bees sting him!'

The three fat servants caught the Little Rooster and threw him into a beehive. But the Little Rooster cried: 'Come, my empty stomach, come, my empty stomach, eat up all the bees.'

His empty stomach ate up all the bees.

He flew back to the window again and cried: 'Cock-a-doodle-doo! Turkish Sultan, give me back my Diamond Button.'

The Turkish Sultan was so mad he didn't know what to do. He called his three fat servants.

'What shall I do with the Little Rooster?'

The first fat servant said: 'Hang him on the flagpole!'

The second fat servant said: 'Cut his head off!'

The third fat servant said: '*Sit* on him!'

The Turkish Sultan cried: 'That's it! I'll sit on him! Catch the Little Rooster and bring him to me!'

The three fat servants caught the Little Rooster and brought him to the Turkish Sultan. The Turkish Sultan opened the wide, wide bag of his trousers and put the Little Rooster in. Then he sat on him.

But the Little Rooster cried: 'Come, my full stomach, let out all the bees to sting the Turkish Sultan.'

His stomach let out all the bees.

And did they sting the Turkish Sultan?

THEY DID!

The Turkish Sultan jumped up in the air.

'Ouch! Ouch! Ow! Ow!' he cried. 'Take this Little Rooster to my treasure chamber and let him find his confounded Diamond Button!'

The three fat servants took the Little Rooster to the treasure chamber.

'Find your confounded Diamond Button!' they said and left him.

But the Little Rooster cried: 'Come, my empty stomach, come, my empty stomach, eat up all the money.'

His empty stomach ate up all the money in the Turkish Sultan's treasure chamber.

Then the Little Rooster waddled home as fast as he could and gave all the money to his poor old mistress. Then he went out into the yard to tell his friends, the insects and worms, about the Turkish Sultan and the Diamond Button.

From *The Good Master*

Nicholas Peabody, the Cobbler

BY URSULA HOURIHANE

Old Nicholas Peabody was the village cobbler. He had a small cottage half-way down the village street where he lived and mended boots and shoes for all the people from the countryside around.

He was a good workman and everyone liked to take their broken-down boots and shoes to Nicholas Peabody because they knew he would patch them up and make a good job of them, somehow, however old they were.

As he worked, Old Nicholas would sing to the boots and shoes. He said it cheered them up and made them feel better. Some people said he was just plain silly, singing and talking away to the boots and shoes.

But all the people who really knew old Nicholas used to whisper among themselves that he was a kind of hobgoblin who had chosen to come and live as a cobbler and had magicked himself into an old man so that he could live in the village like a real person. They said the songs he sang were magic spells to make the boots and shoes get mended faster and better.

One thing was certainly odd. Although he had lived there as long as anyone could remember, Nicholas Peabody never seemed to get any older. He just *stayed old*.

Well, whether he was a hobgoblin or not doesn't really matter. He mended the boots and shoes better than anyone else in the neighbourhood and he never charged people more money than he thought they could pay. In fact, very often, he wouldn't charge anything for his work.

No wonder his shop shelves were always full of boots and shoes that needed mending.

Now it happened one Christmas Eve that Nicholas Peabody's shelves seemed fuller than ever.

'It'll likely be on account of the rough weather we've had lately,' old Nicholas said to himself as he came down that morning and saw all the worn-down and bedraggled-looking boots and shoes waiting to be mended.

'All the same,' he said with a sigh, 'I don't see how I can get that lot done in time for closing at six o'clock. And then it's Christmas, and of course I'll not be working. I'd better do the most important ones first, for the people that need them most.'

He set to work as fast as he could go.

Hammer-tap! Hammer-tap! Stitch, stitch, stitch! went the old cobbler, and he sang as he worked.

'Rap and tap! Rap and tap!
Heel and toe!
Here a stitch, there a stitch,
We must go.
Boots and shoes. Boots and shoes.
Worn and old,
Soon you'll be tidily
Heeled and soled.
Up the streets, down the streets,
Rain or shine;
At your ease, as you please.
There, that's fine!'

So sang the old cobbler as he worked away in the dim light of his little shop.

Jangle-jangle went the bell on his little door as the busy Christmas shoppers hurried in to fetch their boots and shoes.

Nicholas Peabody never even stopped for his usual pipe and cup of tea after the thick bacon sandwich that was all he had time to eat for his dinner.

At last it was six o'clock and the shelves were empty, except for two pairs of boots and two pairs of slippers that no one had been to collect.

'Well,' cried the old cobbler as he bolted his door, put away his tools, and hung up his leather apron, 'I managed to finish every one of the jobs I had to do. What a pity those four pairs must be left idle all over Christmas.'

He went to look at the four pairs of boots and shoes sitting neatly on the shelves.

'Mm,' he said thoughtfully. 'Those boots are young Joe the cowman's, I remember. Reckon he'll have been too busy to call for them, with snow on the ground and all the animals needing feeding and seeing to. And I know he wanted them badly. He said so when he brought them in.'

Nicholas Peabody looked at the other pair of boots. They were much smaller than the cowman's. They belonged to a schoolboy named David.

'Mm,' said old Nicholas, sucking at his empty pipe. 'If this snow lasts, young David's going to need those rough, tough boots. I wonder why he didn't call in for them. Something special must have kept him, I reckon.'

Then he looked at the shoes on the shelf below.

'Miss Perkins's best slippers, surely?' he thought. 'Now, she lives alone and I don't suppose she'd get out in this snow, poor old dear. Perhaps no one was in to do her shopping today.

She'll be upset, not to have her best slippers for Christmas Day. Dear, dear!'

When he looked at the last pair of slippers, Nicholas Peabody had to smile.

They were very small scarlet sandals, and Polly, the milkman's little girl, had broken the strap of one. The old cobbler had fixed a fine new strap that would last till the sandals were outgrown, anyway.

'Dearie me,' he clucked. 'What's little Polly going to do with no scarlet sandals to dance round the Christmas tree? I'll have to do something about all this.'

He thought and he thought. Then a smile crept over his crinkled old face.

'Of course!' he cried. 'It's Christmas Eve and all sorts of magic can work on Christmas Eve. They shall have their boots and shoes, bless them! They shall have them!'

Then the old cobbler went into his back kitchen where Mustapha, his ginger cat, lay stretched in front of the glowing fire.

'Mustapha!' he cried. 'I've a job for you. Wake up, you lazy good-for-nothing! Wake up!'

173

The ginger cat winked and blinked and stretched himself. Then he yawned.

When Nicholas Peabody told him what he wanted him to do, Mustapha arched his back and lashed with his striped tail in horror. Go out in the cold damp snow, indeed? He wasn't at all pleased.

'Come now, Mustapha,' the old cobbler told him. 'It's Christmas Eve, remember. You wouldn't want to be disagreeable on Christmas Eve, would you?'

'Miaou!' said Mustapha. And it really didn't sound very cheerful.

However, Nicholas Peabody fetched a small jar from the mantelpiece, unscrewed the lid, and took out a pinch of blue powder. He dropped a grain or two of the powder on each pair of boots and shoes.

Then the strangest thing happened.

The boots and shoes jumped plop to the ground and lined up neatly, in pairs, behind the ginger cat.

The cobbler opened his front door and peered out. He looked up the street and down. There wasn't a soul in sight.

'Come along now!' he called back over his shoulder, and out through the open door and into the snowy street marched Mustapha, followed by the heavy boots of Joe the cowman, the tough, rough boots of David, the schoolboy, the pointed best shoes of Miss Perkins, and – last of all – the small scarlet sandals of Polly, the milkman's little girl.

'Away you go!' cried Nicholas Peabody, and he watched them set off over the crisp white snow that shone in the moonlight.

Plump-plump-plump went the big heavy boots of Joe the cowman. *Plop-plop-plop* went the rough, tough boots of David

the schoolboy. *Niminy-piminy, trip-trip-trip* went Miss Per-kins's best pointed slippers. *Hop-skip-jump* went the scarlet sandals of Polly, the milkman's little girl.

But Mustapha, the ginger cat, marched in front softly, softly, without a sound.

Presently they came to the little red brick house where Miss Perkins lived.

'Miaou!' cried Mustapha, and the boots and shoes stood quietly in the snow. Mustapha poked Miss Perkins's pointed slippers with his forepaw and they pattered – *niminy-piminy, trip, trip, trip* – up to the neat front door.

Mustapha rattled the letter-box with a great clatter. Then he hurried back to the waiting boots and shoes and marched them off again.

At the gate-post, Mustapha peeped round with his big yellow eyes and he saw Miss Perkins peering out in the darkness.

'Bless me! There are my best slippers, all nicely mended and as good as new for Christmas Day. Thank you, Nicholas Peabody! Thank you.'

She picked up the slippers and shut the front door.

Mustapha and the boots and shoes went on their way. *Plump-plump-plump, plop-plop-plop, hop-skip-jump, softly softly,* over the crisp white snow.

Presently they came to the house where David, the school-boy, lived.

'Miaou!' cried Mustapha and the boots and shoes stood quietly in the snow. Mustapha poked David's rough, tough boots with his white forepaw and they plodded *Plop-plop-plop* up to the front door.

Mustapha banged the door knocker with a great clatter. Then he hurried back to the waiting boots and shoes and marched them off again.

At the gatepost, Mustapha peeped round with his big yellow eyes and he saw David's round rosy face looking out into the darkness.

'Goody me! there are my boots, all nicely mended and as good as new for Christmas Day. Thank you, Nicholas Peabody! Thank you.'

He snatched up the boots and shut the front door.

Mustapha and the boots and shoes went on their way: *plump-plump-plump, hop-skip-jump, softly, softly,* over the crisp white snow.

Presently they came to the cottage where Polly, the milk-man's little girl, lived.

'Miaou!' cried Mustapha and the boots and shoes stood quietly in the snow.

Mustapha poked Polly's little red sandals with his white forepaw and they scampered, *hop-skip-jump*, up to the front door.

Mustapha sprang high and pulled at the string that worked the door-bell – *jingle-jangle!*

At the wicket-gate Mustapha peeped round with his big yellow eyes and he saw Polly's laughing face looking out into the darkness.

'Mummy! Mummy! my red sandals have come. They're all mended and shiny, ready for Christmas Day. Thank you, Nicholas Peabody! Thank you.'

She picked up the sandals and shut the door.

Mustapha and the cowman's boots went on their way: *plump-plump-plump, softly, softly*, over the crisp white snow.

Presently they came to the farm where Joe the cowman lived.

'Miaou!' cried Mustapha, and the boots stood quietly in the snow.

Mustapha poked the cowman's big boots with his white fore-paw and they stumped, *plump-plump-plump*, round to the farmhouse door.

The farmhouse door stood ajar and a beam of light streamed out into the darkness.

'Miaou!' called Mustapha. 'Miaou!'

'There's some poor cat out in the snow,' cried a voice from within. 'It would surely like a saucer of warm milk on such a night.'

Joe the cowman came to the door with a saucerful of warm white milk in his hand.

'Why, 'tis Mustapha, old Nicholas Peabody's cat!' he cried. Then he saw his boots and his eyes grew wide with surprise. 'And here are my great boots,' he said. 'All mended and patched, ready for me to wear. Thank you, Nicholas Peabody! Thank you.'

'Miaou! Thank you, too,' said Mustapha as he lapped up the last of the milk. Then he waved his long tail and trotted off through the crisp white snow, *softly, softly*, home to his own warm fireside.

From *Traveller's Joy*

The Bus Who Had No Upstairs

BY JOHN HOPKINS

Once, not so many years ago, there was just one single-decker bus left in the bus garage. Most of the double-decker buses were fond of the little single-decker and called him 'Shorty' because he had no upstairs. But some of the new Routemasters, who were a bit snobbish, turned up their noses when he chugged past and grumbled when his exhaust pipe puffed out blue smoke.

Because he was the last single-decker, Shorty was rather important. He was the only bus left who could get under the bridges on the road that ran to Little Folliwick, a village about ten miles from the town. All the people of Little Folliwick had to ride in Shorty to get to the shops in the town and as the road ran under two low railway bridges and down narrow lanes with sharp corners, Shorty was the only bus who could manage the journey. Four times a day Shorty travelled to and from Little Folliwick, once in the morning to bring the workers in to the railway station, once in the middle of the morning to fetch the ladies in to do their shopping, once after dinner to take them back, and once again to take the workers home in the evening.

Shorty liked making the journey through the green leafy lanes in the summer, when the hedges sent out long branches to tickle his sides. He enjoyed slipping his way through the winter's ice and feeling the sting of the rain on his roof. One winter when the snow was really deep, he wasn't able to get through at all. Next day a snow-plough cleared a narrow path for Shorty. On his first journey that day he carried not passengers but parcels of food and crates of milk for the people of Little Folliwick. On that day Shorty felt quite a hero. But winter and summer he was glad that he didn't have to run about the crowded sooty town streets all day long like the other buses.

One day in the early summer Shorty was rather sleepily making his afternoon run. He had only a few passengers since most of the ladies had stayed in Little Folliwick for the school sports day. As he rounded one of the sharp bends, his driver had to put on his brakes in a great hurry. There, standing in the middle of the road, were two men with long tape measures and things that looked like telescopes standing on three legs.

Shorty's driver poked his head out of his cab.

'Why don't you have a man with a red flag round the corner to warn people!' he said. 'You'll get run over like that. What are you doing anyway?'

'Sorry, Driver,' answered one of the men. 'We are surveyors measuring up for the new road.'

'New road? I haven't heard anything about a new road.'

'Oh, yes,' said the Surveyor. 'There are going to be a lot of new houses built out at Little Folliwick. A great many new people will be living there. One little single-decker bus won't be able to carry them all. So there is going to be a new road wide enough for double-deckers.'

'But what about the railway bridges? Double-deckers can't get under those,' said Shorty's driver who was rather cross because nobody had told him before.

'Oh, the new road will have bridges *over* the railway,' answered the Surveyor, 'so that's no trouble.'

Shorty drove carefully past the surveyors. As he went on his journey he worried about what he had heard. If there were going to be a lot of new houses and a lot more people and if there was going to be a new road with bridges over the railway and no sharp corners, what was going to happen to him? Perhaps the surveyors would change their minds if they saw how efficiently he did his job and how fond his passengers were of him.

But no! Each day he made his journeys he saw more and more workmen with tractors and bulldozers, picks and shovels, wheelbarrows and red lamps, all of them working on the new road. Each day as he looked over the hedges he could see glimpses of the shining white concrete road, curving in a very important way across the fields. Because the new road was being built, the Council didn't bother to mend the old one and his journey became more and more bumpy, so that even the passengers who had been fond of him began to grumble and to say, 'I wish they would hurry up with that new road. This bus gets more and more uncomfortable.' On the road Shorty was often stuck behind builders' lorries full of cement and stones for the new road. This made him late and each time the Inspector grumbled at his driver.

Finally one day in the autumn as he was standing in the garage getting ready for his first journey of the day, one of the mechanics came out with a pot of paste and stuck a notice on the glass at the back of Shorty's driver's cab.

CLOSING OF SERVICE
'After Monday, 1 October, this bus service will no longer run. Double-decker buses will run every quarter of an hour along the new road.

All the passengers read the notice as they got on the bus and even Shorty couldn't blame them when they seemed pleased. After all, he certainly couldn't do the journey every quarter of an hour, however fast he travelled.

On Monday, 1 October, Shorty stood at the back of the garage and, for the first time that he could remember, nobody came near him. His driver and conductor had taken out one of the double-deckers and had been too excited to think about their old friend. The mechanics hadn't opened his bonnet or pumped up his tyres because they knew he had no journey to make. For about a week he stood there feeling very lonely.

Then the garage Supervisor came and said to Shorty: 'We've got to find a job for you. Can't have you standing about idle. You can collect all the early-morning drivers and conductors and bring them to the garage in time for the first buses and you can take the drivers and conductors of the last buses home late at night.'

Shorty didn't like his new job at all. To tell the truth, the one thing he hated was being woken up early on winter mornings, often when it was still dark. Then, just when he was feeling tired and sleepy at night, he had to go out again. Because he had no regular driver, nobody looked after him and his paint got scratchy, his cushions were full of dust, and his engine began to hiccup.

Sometimes in the spring he was lent out to take parties of children to the seaside. Although he liked to hear the children laughing and shouting with excitement, children can be careless with their ice-cream and sometimes they bounce up and down very hard on the springs. Shorty didn't really enjoy these outings.

Then one day he broke down. Right in the middle of taking a party of rather plump ladies in flowered hats to a meeting in the next town, he broke down. It was a hot day and, by the time a breakdown lorry came to get him going again, the plump ladies were very cross and when they got home they made a Complaint.

The next day the Garage Supervisor came to see Shorty. 'It's no good, Shorty,' he said, 'we've had a Complaint. Your paint-work is not so smart now, your cushions are dirty, and even your engine is not too reliable. I'm afraid you'll have to be sold.'

So Shorty was parked in the yard outside the garage with a big notice saying FOR SALE standing on his bonnet. Each day that nobody bought him, the mechanics had to push him back into the garage for the night. They found this hard work and the Head Mechanic, who was a bit short-tempered, muttered something about 'going on the scrap heap'. Shorty was really worried.

Then one day, in the middle of the summer, a man read the notice and stopped to look at Shorty. Strangely enough he didn't seem too worried about the state of his engine, but walked up and down outside the bus with a folding ruler measuring how long and how wide everything was, and

183

writing all the figures down on the back of an envelope. When he had finished, he went into the Supervisor's office and, although Shorty could see the man and the Supervisor talking, he couldn't hear what they were saying, however hard he tried.

The next day the man came again, bringing his jolly-looking wife and two children, a girl and a boy whom Shorty guessed to be about six and seven years old. This time the man and his wife went into the Supervisor's office while the children climbed in and out of Shorty. Through the office window Shorty could see the man counting out pound notes and giving them to the Supervisor. He knew then that he had been sold! He felt very excited but he wasn't sure whether he was pleased or not. The idea of leaving the garage where he knew everybody and going to live somewhere strange rather scared him. Anyway, only bus companies could run buses, so how could this man and his family run a bus?

The next day the family came again. The Supervisor handed over all Shorty's papers to the man, saying: 'There you are, Mr Black. We were rather fond of Shorty here at the garage, so we're glad to know he's going to have a good home.'

'We'll look after him, don't worry,' answered Mr Black, climbing up into the driver's cab. He started Shorty's engine and drove him carefully out of the garage. Shorty tried to make his engine run as smoothly as possible and he managed not to hiccup. Mrs Black and the two children sat on the long seat at the back of the bus. 'I think we'll call the bus Shorty, too,' said the little boy. 'Yes,' agreed his sister. 'Say "Good-bye" to the garage, Shorty – you won't be seeing it again.'

The road that Mr Black took was the one Shorty used on his way to the seaside with the children's outings, but when they reached the seaside town, instead of parking in the car park the Blacks drove the bus up the steep road that led to the cliffs. At the top Mr Black stopped on the road while Mrs Black got down and opened a wooden gate into a field. Very carefully Mr Black drove Shorty through the gate and parked him on the grass. It was a beautiful field right on the edge of the cliff. The grass was short and covered in daisies. The hedges were thick and smelled sweet with wild roses. There was a wonderful view over the cliff down into the harbour and Shorty could see the sands below and the ships at sea.

Mr Black got down from the cab and stood with his family staring at Shorty. 'Well, well, children,' said Mrs Black, 'this is our new home. Daddy and I have a lot of work to do on Shorty yet, but in about two weeks' time we can all move in.'

Shorty could hardly believe his ears. This was something he'd never heard of. A family living in a bus!

But that is exactly what happened. For two weeks Mr and

Mrs Black worked very hard. Some of Shorty's seats they took out altogether and some they moved round to make beds. Mr Black drilled a hole in Shorty's roof to take the chimney of a small stove and gave him a gleaming coat of red paint. Mrs Black hung pretty curtains at Shorty's windows and planted flowers round his wheels. The children collected round white stones from the bottom of the cliff and made a winding path from the gate to Shorty's door.

So next time you go to the seaside and look up to the top of the cliff, you may well see Shorty and the Black family living very happily together.

Cheep!

They have found my ledge.   They fly so light,
'*Cheep!*' they say, '*cheep!*'   They light so quick,
Round the edge   With all their might
Of the curtain I peep,   Saying '*Cheep!*' as they pick,
Standing quite still   '*Cheep! cheep! cheep!*'
Whenever one comes   In thanks and faith,
To the window-sill   While I stand and peep
For the new-strewn crumbs.   And hold my breath.

ELEANOR FARJEON

The Acrobat in the Lilac Tree

BY IRENE BYERS

The lilac tree was thick with purple bud clusters, and from its topmost branch a small bird watched the starlings quarrelling with the blackbirds for titbits, and listened to the sharp crack of snail shells, as the thrushes knocked them against stones on the rockery. It was Billy the Blue-tit, or Blue Titmouse as he was properly named.

Billy was a handsome bird, with a black beak and a little cap of azure-blue feathers. Blue feathers adorned his wings and tail, and there were touches of pale yellow and green about his body. Billy's bright eyes twinkled as he watched the other birds. He had no need to search for worms and insects, for his breakfast already dangled from a branch on the lilac tree. His keen eyes had also seen something else, for lodged in the branches was a wooden box, and Billy intended to persuade his wife to nest in it.

'Pim-im-im,' he called suddenly in his pretty tinkling voice, as the starlings rushed at the sparrows. 'Pim-im-im, what bad-tempered birds you are to be sure.'

The thrushes stopped looking for snails, the blackbirds paused in their hunt for worms, and the starlings let the sparrows grab a morsel of bread from under their very beaks.

'So it's you, Blue-tit,' one of them called out. 'What are you doing in our garden?'

'I'm looking for a summer home,' Billy replied, 'and I've found one in the lilac tree.'

'We don't want strangers here,' called out a big starling

rudely. 'It's bad enough putting up with the sparrows. Go back to the country where you belong.'

'That's right,' joined in the thrushes. 'We've had a hard enough job feeding ourselves in winter, and you don't belong to the garden.' And forgetting their quarrel, the birds flew at Billy to chase him away. Billy, however, had courage, and merely flew to the top of an apple tree.

'Chur! Chur!' he cried in his scolding voice. 'I tell you the lilac tree is mine, and I'll prove it to you.'

'How?' asked the blackbird sharply.

'You see that lovely half of a coconut hanging from a string? Well, if any of you can eat it, I'll go back to the country.'

'Pooh, that's easy,' said the thrush. 'Watch me.'

The thrush flew to the branch and tried to reach the prize, but his efforts were in vain. Always the coconut dangled beyond his reach.

'Let me try,' said the starling.

If anything, the starling was more clumsy than the thrush, and not one scrap of nut reached his beak. At last, when all the birds in the garden had failed, a sparrow remarked: 'I don't believe it is meant to be eaten at all.'

'Oh, yes it is,' replied Billy.

With a flash of blue wings he reached the lilac tree and, to the amazement of all, the clever little acrobat clung to the nut upside down and pecked hungrily. Next, he swung himself underneath, and all the time his sharp beak was digging deeper and deeper into the sweet, white nut.

'Delicious!' he chirped. 'Simply delicious. If you only knew what a treat you were missing.'

'Well!' exclaimed the blackbird. 'Fancy being able to eat upside down. That really is clever.'

Billy walked round and round the nut and finally perched on the top.

'Does this prove that the lilac tree is mine?' he asked.

All the birds agreed that it did, and with a loud 'Pim-im-im' of triumph, Billy flew away to fetch his mate.

Soon, the wooden box held a cosy nest made of moss, wool, hair, and feathers, and by the time the lilac was in full bloom, seven little white eggs splashed with light red lay inside it. Sometimes the coconut was exchanged for bacon rinds, or lumps of suet, but Billy liked them all equally well, and every morning his rippling, tinkling 'Pim-im-im' could be heard above the notes of the thrushes and the noisy cacklings of the starlings. But although they knew Billy was teasing them, the birds were wiser now and left him alone. If Billy had forgotten the coconut, they had not, and all of them remembered how silly they had felt trying to catch a breakfast that dangled from the end of a string.

From *Our Outdoor Friends*

Two Green Caterpillars

BY MARY COCKETT

After Jan had told Billy how to find food for his pets, they became good friends. They often met in the market, especially at closing time. They were there together one day when Billy picked up a cabbage.

'Look at that!' he said. 'I don't wonder it's been thrown down. It's full of holes.'

'Cabbage caterpillar,' said Jan. 'That's what made those holes. I wonder if there's one still there.'

Just as he spoke, a bright green caterpillar fell to the ground. At least it fell on to a bundle of soft pink tissue paper.

Jan picked it up and put it on the palm of his hand.

'Goodness, it *is* tickly,' he said.

On the ground was a long, thin strip of wood from a grape box. Jan arranged it to rest on two orange boxes so that it made a bridge. He placed the caterpillar on it very carefully.

'There now,' he said to it, 'I bet you've never seen a bridge that length before, have you?'

But the caterpillar said nothing. It was Billy who spoke.

'You lucky thing!' he said. 'I wish I had a caterpillar.'

'I expect there's one somewhere,' said Jan. 'You watch mine and see that it doesn't fall off its bridge.'

Jan peered round among the pile of papers and leaves on the ground. He found a pencil: it was only half as long as his thumb, but he put it in his pocket.

He found an empty matchbox with the picture of a lovely,

cream-coloured castle on it. He had no such label in his collection.

'Hurry up, Jan. This caterpillar of yours takes a lot of watching.'

The matchbox went to join the pencil and the many other things in Jan's pocket. Then he picked up the cabbage with the holes in it. He began stripping off the leaves and looking at them on both sides. As he pulled off the third leaf, he smiled at what he saw inside it.

'Here you are, Billy,' he said. 'Got one.'

Billy's caterpillar raised its head and moved it from side to side in a proud sort of way. Both boys laughed and Jan said, 'So sorry to disturb you, ma'am.'

Then he looked at his own caterpillar. It was peeping over one side of the strip of wood. He picked it up lovingly.

'You'll fall,' he said. 'I say, Billy, shall we have a race with our caterpillars?'

'Yes, let's,' said Billy, 'only yours is a bit bigger than mine and more wriggly. It'll probably get on faster. Yes, I think it's sure to win.'

'It doesn't matter that it's bigger,' said Jan. 'It's fatter too, so it has more weight to carry.'

'Come on then,' said Billy.

Very carefully they held their caterpillars between finger and thumb.

'Start on "Pepper",' said Jan.

Billy nodded. He knew just what Jan meant because it was a way they used at school sometimes for starting games.

Bending side by side over the 'bridge', they said together, 'Salt, mustard, vinegar, PEPPER!'

On that word 'Pepper', they placed the caterpillars exactly

together at the beginning of the bridge. They were a little surprised when the race did not begin at once. It wasn't quite that the caterpillars were refusing to do as the boys told them. They just looked at one another as if to say, 'Fancy seeing you here, my dear! I haven't the slightest idea what's going on, have you?'

'Oh!' groaned the boys. 'They won't race.'

But just then the caterpillars decided that they would. They arched themselves up and then flattened themselves out: arch up, flat down, arch up, flat down....

'Good, good, they're going,' said the boys.

Each, in a loud whisper, cheered on his caterpillar. All went well for about six inches, and then, for no reason that the boys could see, the caterpillars decided to stop.

They put their heads together, and Jan and Billy watched and waited. It was just as though one caterpillar was whispering in the other's ear. Then together they started to turn round. It was as though they had said, 'This is a dull sort of road. Not

194

a spot of green in sight! And so hard on the feet! Let's go back and find another way.'

But alas the bridge was narrow, and the thinner caterpillar lost its balance as it turned.

'Oh, it's fallen,' cried Billy, and it had.

'It won't be hurt,' said Jan. 'It must have had a soft fall here.'

He picked up his own caterpillar for safety, and then bent down with Billy. Below the bridge was a mass of crumpled orange papers: there were wood shavings and bits of boxes, and cabbage leaves, and brussel tops, and string. Somewhere amongst all that was a rather thin green caterpillar.

'I'm going to find it if I stay all night,' said Billy. 'I'm not going to leave it to be swept up.'

'I'll help you,' said Jan.

Together they searched with the greatest care among the market rubbish. They were so serious they might have been looking for gold. They were far too busy to notice that now from across the way a policeman was watching.

Very soon Billy let out a whoop of joy.

'Got it! Got it!' he shouted.

Quickly he put the caterpillar in the hollow of his left hand, and then he made a little roof with his right hand. Both boys were very happy. It was at that point that the policeman strode across.

Kindly, but as though he meant to have an answer, he said, 'What have you got there?'

'Nothing,' said Billy.

Jan, who knew that lots of things were lost in the market, said, 'What's been lost today?'

'I haven't heard yet,' said the policeman. 'No doubt I shall, but just now I want to know what you've found.'

'It's nothing that *belongs* to anybody,' said Jan. 'Truly it isn't.'

'Now, now,' said the policeman. '*Everything* belongs to *somebody*.'

Jan and Billy laughed out loud. Now who could you say an ordinary green caterpillar belonged to?

The policeman realized that there was a little joke against him, but he couldn't think what it could be.

Jan and Billy knew that often when a valuable object was lost, a present of money, or a reward of some kind, was given to the honest person who found it and gave it back.

Billy said, 'There'll be no reward for this.'

He lifted his right hand, and from the hollow of his left the green caterpillar raised its head.

It was the policeman's turn to chuckle now.

'Dear me,' he said, 'I don't wonder you were laughing at me. No, I'm afraid there's no reward for finding a cabbage caterpillar. And there was I thinking that you'd found at least one of the Crown Jewels! Better luck next time!'

From *Seven Days with Jan*

The Skylark

BY LEILA BERG

Once upon a time there was a little girl who sang very prettily. 'Tra-la-la,' she went, 'tra-la-la.' And everyone said, 'My oh my, she sings like a skylark.'

Wherever she went, the little girl only opened her mouth, only let the breath come gently out with a song, and everyone said : 'What a wonder she is, the little lark !'

So one day the little girl went into a field to show the sky-larks. 'I'll show them,' she thought. 'I'll show the skylarks I can sing quite as well as they can. Everyone says so. So that's how it must be.'

Very soon she saw a skylark, a dull brown bird and not at all gay. The little girl smoothed out her blue-and-yellow frock, and patted her golden hair. 'My goodness !' she thought, '*he* doesn't look important.'

The skylark walked along the ground, then he ran a little way. 'Why, he doesn't even hop,' thought the little girl. 'What a *very* dull bird he is indeed.' And she cleared her throat, getting ready to sing.

Suddenly the lark leaped into the air. Beating his strong wings, up he flew, head to the wind. And he sang ! How he sang !

The little girl sang 'I had a little nut tree'. Very prettily she sang it, clear and neat. And when she stopped, she cocked her head on one side, as she did when the people clapped and nodded to her. But the lark went on singing.

Like a little stream trickling over pebbles, the lark went on

197

singing. So the little girl sang 'Baa baa black sheep', and 'Polly put the kettle on'. She scarcely stopped at all, but went straight on from one to the other, wanting to show the lark who was best. But the lark, high up now in the sunshine, the lark went on singing.

Then the little girl began to worry. She sang 'Looby Loo', and 'London Bridge', and even 'Nuts in May', which was a song she didn't care for at all without the game that goes with it. But she had no time to stop and think, for the lark was high up, higher and higher every minute. And the lark went on singing.

Gaily he sang, strongly he sang. He sang as if his mouth was wet and cool, and the notes came bubbling out, tippling and gurgling out of his mouth, and falling into the wind.

Down in the field the little girl sang every song she knew. It was not so neat now, the little girl's song. The notes were

slurred, and slipped about when they should have stood firm and steady and in the song like soldiers. But the little girl didn't care. She stood and sang with her face turned up to the sky. And the tears rolled down her cheeks, for the silly things people had told her.

And now the lark was out of sight. The tiny speck that was a lark flying into the sky had gone, and there was nothing but blue and white, and a dazzling in the little girl's eyes.

'Now it is finished,' she thought. 'It is finished. The lark has stopped singing, and so have I.' And she dropped to the ground, and pressed her cheeks into the grass, and the earth made smudges out of her tears. But the lark, the lark went on singing.

He sang for no one to see, and all the town to hear. He trilled and warbled as if he were filled to the brim with music, and the notes ran over for only the wind to catch. He sang as if the song would never end. And the little girl, quiet now, listened.

Only the lark's song fell down, through the morning. No one clapped. No one chattered. The lark sang quite alone, over a quiet field, and out of a quiet sky. And the little girl listened as if she had never heard real music before.

Now she raised her head. And the lark came in sight again. The little black speck was in the sky again, larger and larger, dropping down. And still the lark was singing.

He dropped lower and lower, sometimes holding on to the wind for a moment, then letting go and dropping again. Now that the speck was bigger, you could see it was a bird, nothing strange or magical or wonderfully changed, just a small brown bird, dropping on the wind into a field.

He sang till he had almost touched the ground. Then he stopped. And he had dropped out of sight.

The little girl did not move. She looked at the grass where

the lark had fallen, and her smudgy face was so still you might have thought she was the little kitchen-maid in the story of the Sleeping Beauty.

So she might have sat for ever, her ears holding the endless echo of the small bird's song.

But just then a foot swished in the grass behind her. And a voice said: 'It's the little skylark, the little skylark, the little girl who sings like a skylark! How lonely you look in the grass.'

But the little girl gave one last look at the clump of grass that held a lark, and she got to her feet. Not a word did she say. Not a sound came out of her mouth. But quiet as quiet, with a trill in her ears, she walked all the way home.

From *The Nightingale and Other Stories*

Snow-white and Rose-red

TRADITIONAL

Once upon a time there was a poor woman who had two daughters, good and beautiful girls. She called them Snow-white and Rose-red after the two rose trees in her garden.

Snow-white was quiet and gentle but Rose-red was a madcap and loved to tease. The two sisters were so fond of each other that they shared everything they had and never quarrelled. The animals in the forest loved them and came to feed from their hands without fear, while the birds sang for joy in the trees.

The girls helped their mother all they could, for she had to work very hard to earn food for them. They kept the house clean and shining and welcomed their mother when she came home from work. Snow-white lighted the fire and had the kettle boiling for tea; Rose-red picked a red rose and a white rose to put on the table, for their mother loved flowers. In the winter they barred the door when it got dark and, while the snow fell outside, the girls went on with their spinning and their mother read wonderful stories to them.

One evening there was a knock on the door.

'Open the door, Rose-red,' said her mother. 'Some traveller must have lost his way and needs shelter.'

Rose-red unbarred the door and in came – a great black bear!

'Oh!' cried the girls in terror and they ran and hid themselves under the bed.

But the bear said in a human voice: 'Don't be afraid! I won't hurt you. I have only come to beg shelter, for it is so cold in the dark forest.'

'You are welcome, friend,' said the mother. 'Lie down by the fire and get warm. Come, my dears, the bear will not hurt you.'

Snow-white and Rose-red crept from under the bed, but still kept at a distance from the shaggy bear.

'Won't you fetch a broom and brush the snow from my coat?' asked the bear.

The girls did so and soon they forgot their fear and did not mind the bear at all. He stayed in the cottage all night and, in the morning, Snow-white opened the door and let him out. He plodded through the deep snow and disappeared into the forest.

After this the bear came every night and the sisters became quite fond of him. They teased him and played games with him and he took it all in good part. At night the door was never barred until the bear was safely indoors.

But when Spring came and the trees were in bud and the birds singing in the forest, the bear bade them good-bye.

'I must go now,' he said, 'for in the good weather the wicked dwarfs who live underground come out and steal anything they can find. I have great treasures which I must guard.'

So Snow-white went with him to the edge of the forest and waved to him until he disappeared among the trees.

One day the girls were gathering firewood. As they searched by a fallen tree, they heard someone muttering angrily. It was an ugly dwarf with fiery red eyes and a white beard as long as your arm. The end of his beard was caught in a cleft in the tree.

'What are you standing there for! Why don't you do something!' he shouted angrily, hopping about in his rage.

'How did you get caught like that?' asked Rose-red.

'It's none of your business!' said the dwarf. 'Help me to free my beautiful beard, can't you!'

The girls tried to pull his beard out of the tree but they could not. In the end Rose-red had to snip off the tip to release him. It was the only way.

How angry the dwarf was! 'How dare you cut off my beautiful beard!' he screamed and he snatched up a sack of gold from near by and disappeared.

'What a comical little man!' said Rose-red, laughing, and the sisters went home.

Not long after, the girls went down to the river to catch a fish for dinner as a surprise for their mother. There they saw someone leaping up and down like a grasshopper. It was the dwarf again. This time his beard was tangled up with his fishing line and a big fish on the end of the line was dragging him into the river.

Snow-white and Rose-red tried to free the dwarf, but the line and the beard were so knotted together that they had to cut off some more of it to free him.

203

The dwarf was not at all grateful. 'How dare you cut off still more of my beautiful beard!' he howled. 'You have made me look a sight!'

He snatched up a sack of diamonds and disappeared and the girls pulled in the fish he had caught and went home.

One fine day their mother asked them to go to town to buy some needles and thread. As they crossed a wide open space, they saw an eagle dart down and snatch something. There was a cry for help and, running up, they found their old friend the dwarf in the talons of the eagle.

Quickly they seized hold of him and tugged and tugged until the eagle had to let go and the dwarf was free.

He did not thank them at all. 'You clumsy things!' he cried in a rage. 'You have torn my coat!' and he seized a sack of precious stones from behind a rock and disappeared.

On the way home, as the sun set, the sisters came upon him again. He did not hear them and they saw that he had spread out a great pile of sparkling diamonds and emeralds and rubies and silver and gold. 'All mine! All mine!' he mumbled over and over again.

When he found that Snow-white and Rose-red were watching him, his anger was terrifying to see. The girls were quite frightened.

'Go away! Go away!' he shouted. 'Don't you dare to touch my treasure.'

Suddenly there was a growl and a roar and there was a big black bear! Before the dwarf could escape, the bear pinned him down with his paw.

'Let me go!' shrieked the dwarf. 'If you are hungry, eat those stupid girls. They are much fatter than I am.'

With one stroke of his paw, the bear put an end to the nasty little creature.

'Snow-white and Rose-red,' he called to the girls who were hiding behind a rock. 'Don't you know me? I am your friend whom you have teased so often.'

The sisters ran towards him happily, but as they came nearer they saw that the great bear had dropped off his furry coat and had become a handsome man, dressed in shining cloth of gold.

'I am a Prince,' he said, taking Snow-white's hand. 'The cruel dwarf had put a spell on me, but it is broken now and I have my own shape again.'

Before long the Bear Prince married Snow-white and his brother married Rose-red. The poor woman, their mother, came to live near her daughters in a beautiful little cottage. In the garden were two rose trees, one of which bore red roses and the other white.

And they all lived happily ever after.

The Good Little Christmas Tree

BY URSULA MORAY WILLIAMS

One snowy Christmas Eve a peasant father walked home through the forest carrying a little Christmas Tree for his children.

It was neither a very tall nor a very fine tree; while the peasant, being a poor man, had no money to deck it about with gold and silver tinsel, dolls, kites, toys, and all the rest, but he did not worry overmuch about it. He knew his wife would discover something in the chest to make the little tree look splendid, and his children, who had never had such a thing in the house before, would be very well pleased.

When he reached home, having tied up the little Christmas Tree in a sack, he bundled it into a corner of the kitchen behind the stove, and nothing that his boy and girl could say or do could persuade him to say a word about it.

They danced about his legs, pointing, peering, and asking a thousand curious questions, while the father only shook his head; but if they approached too close to the stove to have a better look at the mysterious bundle he shouted out: 'Take care! Take care! There is a wolf in the sack!' till they ran to hide themselves behind their mother with little shrieks of terror and excitement.

Presently they grew tired of teasing and went to bed; and when the father and mother were sure that both slept soundly they took the Christmas Tree out of the corner, and set it in a pot, where the mother hung among its branches a number of little brown cookies that she had baked, tied with scarlet thread out of the chest.

The little tree looked very proud and fine, and at first the peasant and his wife admired it with all their hearts, but little by little doubt crept in, for like all parents they wished the best for their little children, and in five minutes they were sighing and shaking their heads like two pine trees on a hill as they said to each other:

'What a pity we have not the smallest silver star nor thread of tinsel to make the branches glitter!'

'How fine a few bright candles would look among the bushy needles! How the children's eyes would sparkle to watch them flicker!'

'How dingy the branches seem! So green and bare! If we had but a few small toys and gifts for our little ones, how they would clap their hands and jump for joy!'

'However, they are good, unselfish children,' the parents agreed, preparing to go to bed; 'they will think the tree very pretty as it is, and make the best of it.'

So off they went, sighing a little, and leaving the little Christmas Tree alone on the kitchen floor.

The tree sighed too, when the peasant and his wife were gone to bed, for they were an honest pair, and he liked their kind and simple hearts. The children, too, were well brought-up and cheerful, deserving the best that could come to them. If he could have crowded his humble branches with stars, diamonds, toys, bright ornaments, and playthings, the little Christmas Tree would have done so in a moment to please so worthy a family, and he stood for a long while thinking deeply, with the cookies in their scarlet threads dangling from his branches like so many little brown mice.

All at once the little tree quivered. One by one he gently pulled his roots out of the pot. He moved so carefully that not a speck of earth fell upon the clean kitchen floor as he moved across to the door and peeped outside.

The snow lay white and deep all round. The pine trees drooped with it, but the world was well awake.

Far up in the Heavenly Meadows the baby Angels were preparing for a party.

There were wolves prowling in the forest, and a pedlar, resting for the night, burned a bright fire to keep them away.

Mass was being sung in the far-off church, while by the light of the moon gnomes and goblins were digging for diamonds under the snow.

Down by the stream a poor boy fished through a hole in the ice, hoping to get something for his supper, and Old Father Christmas, whom the peasants sometimes call St Nicholas, came walking through the forest with a sack over his shoulder.

The little Christmas Tree closed the door quietly behind him,

running out into the snow with the cookies on his branches bobbing up and down like little brown mice as he hurried along.

He ran into a clearing where the gnomes and goblins were digging for diamonds. So busy were they that scarcely one looked up to notice him.

'What will you take for a few of your diamonds?' the little Christmas Tree asked the nearest goblins.

'Ten green needles! Ten green needles!' said the goblins, who used Christmas-tree needles for threading their necklaces of precious stones.

But when the little Christmas Tree had handed over his needles and had received three diamonds in exchange, the goblins suddenly caught sight of the cookies hanging on his branches, and called out:

'Ten green needles and a round brown cookie!'

Now the little Christmas Tree did not intend to part with any of the cookies the peasant mother had made for her children, but in order to pacify the goblins he had to give them first another ten, and then a further dozen, of his green needles, after which he left them and trotted on his way, with the diamonds sparkling among his branches and the cookies bobbing up and down like little brown mice.

When he had left the goblins far behind he came on a circle of scarlet toadstools, so bright and splendid with their red tops all spotted with white that he knew it would delight the children to see a few peeping from among his needles.

But he had hardly helped himself to a handful before he heard a terrible baying, which came nearer and nearer and nearer. Surrounding him was a ring of wolves, their tongues hanging out, their eyes green and hungry.

'Don't you know better than to pick scarlet toadstools?' they asked the little Christmas Tree. 'Don't you know that every time you pluck one a bell rings in the Wolves' Den?'

'What will you take for your red toadstools?' the little Christmas Tree asked, trembling with fear.

'Twenty green needles! Twenty green needles!' said the wolves, who used Christmas-tree needles for picking thorns out of their paws. But when the little tree had plucked out the needles they noticed the cookies hanging among his branches, and growled out:

'Twenty green needles and two brown cookies!'

Now the little Christmas Tree did not intend to let the wolves have any of the cookies the peasant mother had baked for her children, so he made one bound out of the circle, shaking a shower of sharp needles into the wolves' faces, sending them howling into the forest. He then went on his way, with the toadstools gleaming, the diamonds glittering, and the cookies bobbing about like little brown mice.

Now he came to a stream out of which all movement seemed frozen. But underneath the ice the fish still swam in the current, and here, beside a bridge hung with silver icicles, a poor boy had made a hole in the ice and was fishing for his supper.

The Christmas Tree was about to cross the bridge when he noticed the icicles, and thought how pretty a few would look hanging from the tips of his boughs like spears.

'What will you take for a few of those icicles?' he asked the fisher-boy.

'They are not mine to sell,' the poor boy replied. 'God made the icicles; I suppose. He means us to take what we please. But pray tread carefully, or you will frighten away my little fishes.'

The little Christmas Tree was so pleased with the boy's courtesy that when he had broken away a few beautiful icicles he handed some of his own green needles to the fisher-boy to make new hooks.

The boy thanked him gratefully, but his eyes strayed so wistfully towards the cookies hanging among the branches that the little tree felt much perplexed. He could not part with any of the cookies the peasant mother had made for her children, but he said: 'If you wish, you may take one bite out of my largest cookie, for I feel sure that is what any mother would wish!'

The boy did eagerly as he was told, and immediately felt as if he had risen from a banquet of roast goose, turkey, venison, plum pudding, mince-pies, jellies, and dessert, while the little Christmas Tree hurried on his way, with the icicles sparkling, the toadstools gleaming, the diamonds glittering, and the cookies bobbing about like little brown mice.

Soon he met a procession of people who were wending their way through the forest to church.

All were carrying candles which they lit as they passed

through the door, where already a great number of people were singing and praising God.

The little Christmas Tree crept in behind them to listen. In the nave stood trees a great deal taller that he, their branches ablaze with coloured candles that flickered as if they too were singing anthems.

The little tree dared not ask for a candle, so he stood close by the door, listening and watching for quite a long while.

Presently an old man and a young girl came into the church. The girl took coloured candles out of her basket, lighted them, and tied them on to the branches of the little Christmas Tree.

'There! That will please the good angels and amuse some poor child on Christmas morning,' said the girl.

But the old man grumbled:

'Look at all those cookies hanging on the branches! They will do no good there! They will go bad! The mice will eat them during the night! They ought to be cut off and given to the poor!'

The little Christmas Tree trembled so much at the old man's words that quite a shower of green needles fell on the floor round the young girl's feet, and, as she and the old man walked up the church to join the singing, the little tree quickly slipped through the door and out into the forest, with the candles flickering, the icicles sparkling, the toadstools gleaming, the diamonds glittering, and the cookies bobbing about like little brown mice.

Soon he had left the church far behind.

Deep in the forest he came upon the pedlar sitting by his dying fire. Beside him all his wares were spread out on the snow – puppets, boats, knives, ribbons, shawls, a fine wooden horse, and a dainty little pair of red slippers.

'What will you take for that wooden horse, and that dainty pair of slippers?' asked the little Christmas Tree.

'Enough wood to make my fire blaze. I am freezing to death!' replied the pedlar.

The little Christmas Tree began to throw handfuls of his green needles into the fire, but they only smouldered. Then he broke off some of his lower twigs. They crackled a little and went out. Then he broke off his best branch, and the fire burst into a bright blaze.

The pedlar gave the wooden horse to the little Christmas Tree, but when he saw the cookies hanging on the branches a greedy look came into his eyes and he said: 'If you want the slippers too, you must give me three of those round brown cookies!'

But the little Christmas Tree did not intend to part with any of the cookies the peasant mother had made for her children.

'Oh no!' said he, 'that was not in our bargain at all! But I will give you another branch to keep your fire alight, and you shall give me the red slippers.'

The pedlar grumbled and complained, but before he could change his mind the little Christmas Tree threw another branch on the fire, picked up the slippers, and ran away with them into the forest, with the wooden horse prancing, the candles flickering, the icicles sparkling, the toadstools gleaming, the diamonds glittering, and the cookies bobbing about like little brown mice.

He ran right into the Heavenly Meadows where the baby Angels were holding their party.

They were so pleased to see him they clustered round him, caressing him with their soft little wings. Their pink toes peeped out from under their white nightgowns, and they clapped their little pink hands together in joy and delight.

When they had danced around him nearly a hundred times they began to tie their brightest stars to his boughs. No wonder the little Christmas Tree glowed with pleasure and gratitude!

He had very few needles left on his branches, but he offered them all as playthings to the baby Angels.

But when they grew tired of playing with the pretty green needles they began to beg for the cookies, stretching out their little hands for them and clamouring, as children will.

Now the little Christmas Tree did not intend to part with any of the cookies the peasant mother had made for her children, but the baby Angels had been so kind to him, and their rosy faces were so beseeching, that he had not the heart to refuse them, so at last he said: 'Each one of you may take a tiny bite out of just one cookie, for I feel sure that is what any mother would wish!'

But when the baby Angels had had one bite they all wanted another, and to escape them the little Christmas Tree had to take to his heels and run until he had left the Heavenly Meadows far behind, with the stars shining, the slippers flapping, the wooden horse prancing, the candles flickering, the icicles sparkling, the toadstools gleaming, the diamonds glittering, and the cookies bobbing about like little brown mice.

He ran till the forest was dark again, and there he found a pool, so deep and so clear that the ice had not covered it at all.

'I will have just one drink of cool water,' said the little Christmas Tree. 'Then I must be going home.'

But when he bent over the pool and saw his reflection in the moonlight he was so overcome by his miserable appearance that he shrank back into the snow as if he wished to hide himself completely.

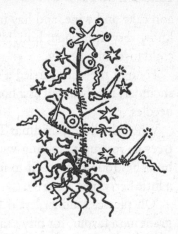

Gone were his bushy needles with their pale green tips, the jaunty fingers outstretched from each sturdy bough. Some of the boughs themselves were gone, leaving jagged, miserable stumps behind.

It was as if the stars, the slippers, the horse, the candles, the icicles, the toadstools, and the diamonds hung on the arms of some ragged scarecrow!

He was ashamed to go home!

While the little Christmas Tree lay almost dying of shame in the snow, someone came tramping through the forest, bringing with him joy and gladness.

St Nicholas is the children's saint. Sometimes they call him Old Father Christmas, and sometimes Santa Claus, and they credit him with all kinds of strange tricks and ways. They say he drives reindeer across the starry skies, halting them on the snowy roofs to dive down chimneys with loads of gifts for stockings, sabots, and shoes. They leave presents for him, milk and cake and wine, and hay in the shoes for his reindeer. They know very little about him, but they say a great deal, and every child loves him dearly.

Tonight the saint carried a splendid Christmas Tree over his shoulder, nearly as tall as a house, and every branch bushy with needles.

When the little Christmas Tree saw him coming through the trees he rose up trembling with shame, huddling his poor bare branches round him as if to make himself out to be as small as a little berry bush close by.

'Oh please, kind sir,' said the little Christmas Tree. 'Please grant me a favour, for pity's sake!'

When St Nicholas stopped to listen to him the little tree began very fast and piteously: 'I beg you, kind sir, to take off my branches the shining stars, the slippers, the wooden horse, the icicles, the toadstools, the diamonds, and, above all, the little cookies tied with scarlet thread, and to tie them on the branches of that splendid tree you carry! Then of your kindness will you take the tree to the cottage at the end of the forest, and leave it at the door? For I have become such a scarecrow,' said the little tree, sobbing, 'that I am ashamed to go home!'

But St Nicholas smiled very kindly at the little Christmas Tree, stroking him with his hand on his poor, bare branches.

At the first touch the tree prickled all over! At the second he had the strangest sensation, as if each twig were bursting and popping open like so many buttons!

His needles were growing again!

As they grew thicker and thicker, new boughs sprang from the torn stumps till, reflected in the forest pool, he now saw a splendid tree, among whose branches shone bright stars and dangled silver icicles.

The candles, slippers, horse, toadstools, diamonds, and cookies were almost hidden behind the wealth of fresh green that covered the tree from top to toe.

'We will go home together!' said Old Father Christmas.

As they walked through the quiet forest they passed the Heavenly Meadows, and all the baby Angels fell in procession behind them. The pedlar left his glowing fire and followed behind the Angels. The people were leaving church. They joined the pedlar, still singing their Christmas hymns. The boy at the frozen stream picked up his basket of silver fish to follow the crowd, while the wolves skulked out of the trees, mild as lambs, trotting with the rest.

The gnomes and goblins put down their picks and shovels to follow the wolves, while in front of them all walked St Nicholas and the little Christmas Tree, with the stars twinkling, the slippers dancing, the wooden horse galloping, the candles flaming, the icicles dazzling, the toadstools shining, the diamonds flashing, and the cookies bobbing about like little brown

mice, each with a tiny bite taken out of it, except the largest, which had two!

The peasant's children were awake and peeping through the window, as children will on Christmas night.

'Look! Look what is coming through the forest! Look at the wolves! Look at the gnomes and goblins! Look at the sweet little Angels in their white nightgowns! Look at the people singing, and the poor boy carrying his basket of fish! Look at the pedlarman! and *look!* ... there is Old Father Christmas, and he is bringing us a little Christmas Tree all covered with ... Oh! quick! quick! get back into bed and pull the bed-clothes over our heads as quick as we can, or we shall never get anything at all!'

The Laughing Dragon

BY RICHARD WILSON

There was once a King who had a very loud voice and three sons. His voice was *very* loud. It was so loud that when he spoke everyone jumped. So they called the country he ruled over by the name of Jumpy.

But one day the King spoke in a very low voice indeed. And all the people ran about and said, 'The King is going to die.'

He *was* going to die, and he *did* die. But before he died he called his three sons to his bedside. He gave one half of Jumpy to the eldest son; and he gave the other half to the second son. Then he said to the third, 'You shall have six shillings and eightpence farthing and the small bag in my private box.'

In due time the third son got his six shillings and eightpence farthing, and he put it safely away into his purse.

Then he got the bag from the King's private box. It was a small bag made of kid, and was tied with a string.

The third son, whose name, by the way, was Tumpy, untied the string and looked into the bag. It had nothing in it but a very queer smell. Tumpy sniffed and then he sneezed. Then he laughed, and laughed, and laughed again without in the least knowing what he was laughing at.

'I shall never stop laughing,' he said to himself. But he did, after half an hour and two minutes exactly. Then he smiled for three minutes and a half exactly again.

After that he looked very happy; and he kept on looking so happy that people called him Happy Tumpy, or H.T. for short.

Next day H.T. set out to seek his fortune. He had tied up the bag again and put it into the very middle of his bundle.

His mother gave him some bread and a piece of cheese, two apples and a banana. Then he set out with a happy face. He whistled as he went along with his bundle on a stick over his shoulder.

After a time he was tired, and sat down on a large milestone. As he was eating an apple, a black cat came along. It rubbed its side against the large stone, and H.T. stroked its head.

Then it sniffed at the bundle that lay on the grass. Next it sneezed, and then it began to laugh. It looked so funny that H.T. began to laugh too.

'You must come with me, puss,' said H.T. The cat was now smiling broadly. It looked up at H.T. and he fed it. Then they went on side by side.

By and by H.T. and the cat came to a town, and met a tall thin man. 'Hallo,' he said, and H.T. said the same.

'Where are you going?' asked the man.

'To seek my fortune,' said H.T.

'I would give a small fortune to the man who could make me laugh.'

'Why?' asked H.T.

'Because I want to be fat,' said the thin man, 'and people always say "laugh and grow fat".'

'How much will you give?' asked H.T.

'Oh, five shillings and twopence halfpenny, anyhow,' said the man.

H.T. put down his bundle and took out his bag. He held it up near the man's face and untied the string. The man sniffed and then he sneezed. Then he laughed for half an hour and two minutes. Next he smiled for three minutes and a half.

By that time he was quite fat. So he paid H.T. five shillings and twopence halfpenny. Then he went on his way with a smile and a wave of his hand.

'That is good,' said H.T. 'If I go on like this I shall make my fortune.' He tied up his bag and went on again. The black cat walked behind him with a smile on his face that never came off.

After an hour the companions came to another town. There were a lot of men in the street, but no women, or boys, or girls. The men looked much afraid.

H.T. went up to one of them. 'Why do you look so much afraid?' he asked politely.

'You will look afraid too, very soon,' said the man. 'The great dragon is coming again. It comes to town each day and takes a man and a cheese. In ten minutes it will be here.'

'Why don't you fight it?' asked H.T.

'It is too big and fierce,' said the man. 'If any man could kill it, he would make his fortune.'

'How is that?' asked H.T.

'Well,' said the man, 'the King would give him a bag of gold and make the Princess marry him.'

All at once H.T. heard a shout.

'The dragon is coming!' called a man who wore a butcher's apron. Then he ran into his shop, banged the door, and threw a large piece of meat out of the window. There was now nothing in the street but H.T., the cat, and the large piece of meat.

H.T. did not run away, not even when he saw the huge dragon come lumbering up the street on all fours. It crept along, and turned its head this way and that. Its face had a terrible look.

Fire came out of its nose when it blew out, and three of the houses began to burn. Then it came to the meat. It sniffed it and stopped to eat it. That gave H.T. time for carrying out his plan.

He took out his bag and untied the string. Then he threw it down before the dragon. On it came, blowing more fire from its nostrils. Soon the butcher's shop was burning. There was a noise like the noise from an oven when the meat is roasting.

The dragon still came on. When it got up to the bag it stopped. It sniffed. Then it sneezed so hard that two houses fell down flat. Next it began to laugh, and the noise was so loud that the church steeple fell into the street.

Of course, the dragon had stopped to laugh. It sat up on its hind legs and held its sides with its forepaws. Then it began to smile. And a dragon's smile, you must understand, is about six feet wide!

The dragon looked so jolly that H.T. did not feel afraid of it any more; not in the least. He went up to it, and took one of its forepaws into his arm. The cat jumped on to the dragon's head. And they all went along the street as jolly as sandboys.

A woman popped her head out of a high window. 'Take the

first to the right,' she said, 'and the second to the left. Then you will come to the King's royal palace. You cannot miss it.'

'Thank you very much,' said H.T.; and he and the dragon and the cat smiled up at her. H.T. waved his hand, the dragon waved its other forepaw, and the cat waved its tail.

So they went on down one street and then another. At last they came to a big, open, green space in which stood a big palace. It had a wall round it with four large gates in it. At each gate there was a sentry-box. But not one sentry could be seen.

H.T., with his friend the dragon, came smiling up to one of the gates. Above the gate H.T. saw someone peeping over the wall. 'He wears a crown,' he said to the dragon, 'so it must be the King.' The dragon kept on smiling.

'Hallo!' said the King. 'What do *you* want?'

'Hallo!' cried H.T. 'I want the bag of gold and the Princess.'

'But you have not killed the dragon,' said the King.

'I should think not,' said H.T. 'Why, he is my friend. He is my very dear friend. He will not do any harm now. Look at him.'

The King stood up and put his crown straight. It had fallen

over one eye in his fright. The dragon went on smiling in his sleepy way. There was no fire in his nose now.

'But,' said the King. 'How do I know he will not begin to kill people again?'

'Well,' said H.T., 'we will make a big kennel for him and give him a silver chain. Each day I will give him a sniff from my empty bag. Then he will be happy all day and go to sleep every night.'

'Very well,' said the King. 'Here is the bag of gold. You will find the Princess in the laundry. She always irons my collars. And you can have my crown as well. It is very hard and heavy. I do not want to be King any more. I only want to sit by the fire and have a pipe and play the gramophone.'

So he threw his crown down from the wall. The dragon caught it on his tail and put it on H.T.'s head. Then H.T. went to the laundry and married the Princess straight away.

And the dragon lived happily ever after, and so did the cat; and so did everybody else – at least, until they died.

I ought to tell you that King H.T. used the bag all his life to keep the dragon laughing. He died at the age of 301 years, one month, a week, and two days. The next day the dragon took such a very hard sniff at the bag that he *died* of laughing.

So they gave the bag to the dentist. And when anyone had to have a tooth out he took a sniff. Then he laughed so much that he did not feel any pain. And when the tooth was out he was happy ever after, or at least until the next time he ate too many sweets.

From *The Ever-Ever Land*

Bed in Summer

In winter I get up at night
And dress by yellow candle-light.
In summer, quite the other way,
I have to go to bed by day.

I have to go to bed and see
The birds still hopping on the tree,
Or hear the grown-up people's feet
Still going past me in the street.

And does it not seem hard to you,
When all the sky is clear and blue,
And I should like so much to play,
To have to go to bed by day?

ROBERT LOUIS STEVENSON

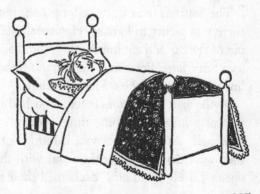

Off to the Sea!

BY EILEEN AND VERA COLWELL

Peter and Joan were counting their pocket money. 'Four shillings,' said Peter.

'I've beaten you,' boasted Joan. 'I've got five!'

Peter and Joan Trent and their mother and father were going to the seaside for a holiday. Now the great day had almost come. Early next morning they would be off!

By six o'clock they were putting the last things in their cases. Downstairs their mother was setting breakfast and cutting sandwiches for their picnic lunch. 'Come along, children,' she called and Peter and Joan flew down, two steps at a time.

Breakfast was over very quickly and soon everything was packed in the car – luggage, picnic basket, Peter's cricket bat, and last year's buckets and spades.

'Good-bye, good old Bess!' they shouted to the dog next door. Bess thumped her tail and looked after them wistfully. Dogs like going away too.

The journey was quite a long one, but the sun shone and there was plenty to look at. However, everyone was glad to get out of the car and eat lunch under the shade of some trees down a country lane. Peter and Joan soon finished theirs – they were impatient to reach the sea and the sands.

In the late afternoon, Peter, who had been hanging out of the car window for some time, suddenly shouted: 'The sea! The sea!' And there it was, shining in the sun. Before long they were driving along the front with the car windows wide open. 'Lovely fresh air!' exclaimed their mother, breathing in

deeply. 'Lovely fresh air!' echoed the children, gulping in air noisily until they could hardly breathe for laughing.

Unpacking didn't take nearly as long as packing had done. 'Can we go down to the sea, Mummy?' begged the children. Away they raced, only stopping when they reached the sands to take off their shoes and socks. The sand felt cool and smooth to their feet and they chased each other into the sea to paddle.

'Oh, it's cold!' cried Joan, dancing up and down at the edge of the water.

'Pooh! It's smashing!' jeered Peter.

But soon it was time for supper and early bed after their long and exciting day. Tomorrow would soon be here.

'Who's going to bathe with me?' asked their father at breakfast next morning.

'I am,' said Peter at once, but Joan wasn't so sure she wanted to. However, before long they were running across the beach, Joan's red bathing costume and Peter's green one, bright against the blue sea.

'Watch me swim!' shouted Peter and splashed and puffed several strokes, but Joan stayed timidly ankle-deep in the water. 'Come along, Joan,' said her father encouragingly. 'I'll hold you up while you try.'

So Joan did try. It was hard work at first, but by the time Mummy called to them to come out, she was splashing happily with a rubber ring to support her.

'I'm frightfully hungry!' complained Peter as his mother helped to rub him dry. 'I could eat a whale!'

'Well, all you'll get is a biscuit,' laughed his mother and in a moment the two children were sitting down quietly, eating biscuits and wriggling their toes in the sand. To their surprise, they felt quite tired.

'How about learning to sail on the lake?' suggested their father in the afternoon. 'We'll hire a boat for an hour or two if you like.'

The little yachts with their red, yellow, white, and green sails, looked very gay. Joan and Peter chose one with a red sail and they all climbed on board. Mr Trent showed them how to steer and how to bring the sail over in order to tack.

'This is smashing!' said Peter, who loved the water. Just at that moment a sudden gust of wind made the yacht heel over and everyone was drenched by a wave.

'Oh dear! I'm wet through!' exclaimed Mrs Trent.

'Don't worry, you won't drown,' said her husband reassuringly as the spray broke over them once more. It happened so many times and the sun was so warm that soon no one minded at all, for it was so exciting.

Each day was fine and sunny and all the family were as brown as berries, for they spent every moment they could on the sands in the salty wind and sunshine. Peter and Joan built

castles in the sand and played games with the other children and before long they had made several friends.

'Let's catch some shrimps for tea,' suggested Peter one day. 'There's a special rock pool where there are lots, Tony says.'

'Do you know the way to the pool?' asked Joan.

'Of course I do,' answered her brother. 'We just go along that path on the cliffs.'

They walked along the narrow track. Sea pinks grew on the edge of the cliff and the seagulls were wheeling and squawking over the sea.

'Isn't *this* the path we ought to take?' asked Joan as they came to a track down.

'No,' said Peter impatiently. 'It's the next one, I'm sure.'

So they turned down the second path. It was very steep and it was difficult to manage their shrimping nets and pails, for they needed a hand to steady themselves by holding on to the rough grass. The sands seemed a long way down and Joan didn't feel too happy.

'It's so steep, Peter,' she said timidly. 'Shall we go back?'

'Don't fuss, Joan! I'm the oldest so I know what I'm doing. Just follow me,' said Peter. However, he took his sister's hand and helped her down the worst bits, for, secretly, he knew he was on the wrong path.

'Oh, my pail has gone!' cried Joan as it clattered down the slope, jumping over rocks and disappearing.

'Don't worry, we shall find it at the bottom,' said Peter. I think I'll send mine after it – it's so difficult to hold everything.' So his pail went rattling down as well.

After that they got on better. There was a sandy slope so they sat down and slid the rest of the way, rolling over and over the last few feet.

'I don't see the pool,' said Joan. Neither could Peter, but just at that moment, he caught sight of his friend, Tony, amongst a group of children, so he ran over to join him. There was the pool at last.

'I knew it was there all the time,' he said.

Soon they were fishing with the other children. Joan soon tired of trying to catch shrimps that disappeared as soon as she looked at them, so she ran off on her own and collected shells and coloured pebbles to take home. Peter went on fishing and, at last, with great pride, he showed Joan three shrimps he had caught in his net.

It was tea time and Joan and Peter hurried home, along the beach this time. Peter took his three shrimps to the landlady. 'They're for tea,' he explained.

'Well, now, what a funny thing you should bring shrimps,' she said. 'I've got some for you as well, so these will help out nicely.'

Everyone enjoyed the shrimp tea, especially Peter, for he was sure he could recognize the three he had caught. 'Mine are pinker than the others,' he explained.

All too soon it was the last night. 'What shall we do?' asked their father.

'Let's go to Pretty Polly's Playground,' begged the children, for they had been longing to go to the children's fun fair all week and had often heard the music blaring out from the roundabouts and swings.

So they all walked along to the fair. Everyone seemed to be shouting, there was a roar of machinery, and crowds of people were strolling about. 'Keep together, children!' cried their mother. 'Hold on to us or we shall lose you.'

'The Aeroplane Roundabout first,' said their father, steering them that way, and soon they were all swinging round faster and faster and higher and higher. 'Supersonic!' shouted Peter, his hair blown in every direction and his eyes shining. But Joan held on tightly to the edge of the aeroplane and hoped it would soon be over. She and her mother felt so dizzy after the ride,

that they chose to walk round the stalls rather than go on anything else.

Peter and his father hurried off to the Car Track and bumped round with great enjoyment. Peter was allowed to steer and he crashed into other cars boldly just for fun. It didn't matter for everyone was doing the same!

They had a shy at the coconuts and Mr Trent threw a ball so hard that he knocked one over. What a fine coconut it was, nice and whiskery and really heavy. Joan was sure that it was the biggest one in the fair!

'Now for the Crooked House!' she pleaded, for this had greatly taken her fancy. The windows were crooked and the floor tipped at all kinds of queer angles, the doors were crooked and there were a great many mirrors everywhere.

'Oh, Mummy, look at that queer-looking girl with crooked legs,' whispered Joan.

'Hush, dear,' began her mother. ... 'It's *you*, Joan!' said Peter laughing. 'Look at *me*!' and there he was in another mirror with long thin legs and a neck like a giraffe.

How they laughed! Each new mirror made them look worse and their mother and father looked funnier than either of them, the children said. They laughed so much that they felt quite weak and had to get out of the Crooked House into the fresh air. There they all sank down on a seat on the promenade. 'That's the best laugh I've had for a long time!' said their mother, wiping her eyes.

That night Peter and Joan dreamed of moving floors and funny-looking people flying in the air, of swimming through the waves and catching shrimps – but the morning came at last and with it the thought of 'Home'.

'I wish we could stay another week!' said Peter as he dressed.

'So do I!' sighed Joan.

The car was packed and they were ready to start. 'Good-bye!' they called as they drove along the sea front and looked across the sands at the white foam on the waves. 'Good-bye!'

'What a smashing holiday!' said Peter.

And they all agreed.

Farmer Comfort Buys a Pig

BY URSULA HOURIHANE

One fine spring morning Farmer Comfort said to his wife, ' 'Tis market day, m'dear, and I'm off to town to buy that pig we've been saving up for so long. Mind the farm well while I'm away and look for me home again by tea time.'

'That I will, love,' said Mrs Comfort, and she fetched his cosy blue muffler and his best hat while he fastened up his shining big boots. 'Good-bye, and be sure you choose a nice friendly pig,' called Mrs Comfort as she waved her handkerchief while Farmer Comfort flicked his whip and set off for market in the trap with Polly the grey mare. Trit-trot! Trit-trot! down the lane they went while the sun shone and all the little birds sang gaily as they darted to and fro with twigs and moss for their new nest homes.

'To market, to market, to buy a fat pig!' sang Farmer Comfort as they jogged along between the green hedges. 'I want one that's friendly and not very big.' He pulled gently at the reins to show Polly it was time to turn to the right and go along the main road to the town. 'Why!' he cried. 'To market, to market, to buy a fat pig; I want one that's friendly and not very big. That's a rhyme, that is! Fancy me making a rhyme, Polly! And all about our new pig, too!' He was so pleased with himself that he sang his little rhyme all over again to a queer little tune he made up as he went along.

> 'To market, to market, to buy a fat pig.
> I want one that's friendly and not very big.'

By the time Farmer Comfort had sung his little rhyme over three times they had reached the outskirts of the town and there were such a lot of cars and carts and buses from the countryside coming into the market that Farmer Comfort had to be very careful where he was going and he thought he'd better not sing any more. 'Whoa back there, Polly!' he said as the traffic lights changed and they had to wait behind another trap before they could get over the cross-roads. There was such a lot of traffic ahead of them that Farmer Comfort knew they might even have to wait again when the lights changed. He watched the trap in front and kept ready to move when the other trap moved. 'HRMMPH! HRMMPH!' grunted a strange sort of voice from the back of the trap in front. Farmer Comfort looked quickly to see who it might be. 'HRMMPH! HRMMPH!' he heard again and a round pinky pig's face peered up at him from under a net that covered the back of the trap in front. 'Bless my soul!' cried Farmer Comfort in surprise. 'And who might you be, I'd like to know?' 'HRMMPH! HRMMPH!' said the pinky pig and its little black eyes seemed to smile at Farmer Comfort. 'Well! you're a nice friendly little creature, I must say,' said Farmer Comfort. Then the traffic lights changed; the

235

trap in front started with a jerk, and the little pink pig disappeared from view. Farmer Comfort and Polly moved on too. 'I must look out for that little pig at the market,' thought Farmer Comfort. 'It's just the kind we're wanting. I'll follow the trap and ask the farmer how much money he wants for his pig.' But oh dear! By the time Farmer Comfort reached the traffic lights they had changed again to red, and that meant, of course, that nothing else could go over till the lights came green again. 'Well, if that ain't a nuisance and a botheration!' cried Farmer Comfort as he saw the trap with the little pink pig disappearing in the distance. 'Now I'll have to hunt around all over the place till I find my little pig and mebbe someone else will have bought it already before I get there. Oh dear! Oh dear!' What a long time it seemed before the lights changed back to green and Farmer Comfort and Polly could hurry across to try to catch up with the little pig.

At last they reached the market place. 'MOO-MOO!' 'BAA-BAA!' 'QUACK-QUACK-QUACK!' 'CHK-CHK-CHK!' they heard on every side. You never heard such a noise. All the farmers were busy tying up their traps and driving the animals they had for sale into the proper pens for all the customers to see. Farmer Comfort tied Polly up in as quiet a corner as he could find and set off to look for the little pink pig.

Presently he saw a crowd of men standing round looking at something. Farmer Comfort hurried over. 'I wonder what they're selling here?' he said to himself. Then he heard 'MOO-MOO! MOO-MOO!' 'It's no good looking here,' thought Farmer Comfort. 'This is all cows and bulls.' And he went on a bit farther.

Presently he saw another little crowd of men standing watching something. Farmer Comfort hurried over. 'I wonder what they're selling here,' he said to himself. Then he heard 'BAA-BAA! MAA-MAA!' 'It's no good looking here,' thought Farmer Comfort. 'This is all lambs and sheep.' And he went on a bit farther.

Presently he saw another little crowd of men watching something. Farmer Comfort hurried over. 'I wonder what they're selling here,' he said to himself. Then he heard 'QUACK-QUACK! CHK-CHK-CHK!' 'It's no good looking here,' thought Farmer Comfort. 'This is all ducks and hens.' And he went on a bit farther.

He looked here, there, and everywhere, but he just couldn't see a sign of any pigs. He was disappointed.

'Well, I may as well go back to Polly and start home,' he said. 'There can't be any pig sale today.' And he turned back sadly and walked through the noisy market till he found his own trap with Polly waiting patiently in her quiet corner.

Farmer Comfort unhitched the reins and climbed up on to his seat. He was just going to tell Polly to Gee-up there! when he heard a strange sound. 'HRMMPH! HRMMPH!' My goodness! Farmer Comfort did jump! And when he looked round quickly to see where the sound came from, what do you think? There, just beside his trap, stood the trap with the little pink pig peeping out from under the net at the back! 'Well! twiddle my whiskers!' cried Farmer Comfort. 'Whoever saw the likes of that?' And he jumped down from his seat and went to talk to the man who had brought the little pink pig to market.

'I was just going to take him home again,' said the man when Farmer Comfort found him. 'Seems there's no pig sale today so 'twas no good my stopping longer.'

And weren't they both pleased they had met each other! But the one who was most pleased was the little pink pig!

> 'I went off to market to buy a fat pig :
> I've got one that's friendly and not very big!'

sang Farmer Comfort as they jogged homewards with the little pink pig safely in the back of the trap. 'HRMMPH! HRMMPH! HRMMPH!' sang the little pink pig. 'HRMMPH! HRMMPH!'

From *Sugar and Spice*

The Little Hare and the Tiger

BY ELIZABETH CLARK

It was ten o'clock on a sunshiny morning – the kind of morning that makes everyone feel happy and cheerful. But no one seemed at all happy or cheerful in the forest that day. The little hare was sitting in an open space among the bushes at the edge of the wood; he was shaking his head and saying over and over again, '*No*, I shall not go. No,' said the little hare, 'I shall not go. *No*,' said the little hare, very firmly and loudly, 'I *certainly* shall not go.'

By his side sat the jackal, who was saying, 'Oh, do go. Do, *do* go. Dear hare, dear, kind, beautiful hare, *do* go.' And each time the jackal spoke the little hare shook his head till his ears flapped, and said, 'No, *no*, I shall *not* go.'

Some of the other animals were peeping anxiously out of the bushes. The deer was there, the buffalo, the porcupine, the fox, the pig, the peacock, and many others. They all seemed very worried; and so too would you have been! Now I will tell you what it was all about.

Some time before this story begins a large and hungry tiger had come to live in the forest. Every day he prowled about looking for food, and every day he killed two or three of the animals. He really killed many more than he needed to eat. Everyone was afraid of him, and no one could feel happy or comfortable.

But one day the jackal had a bright idea – at least it seemed bright to him. He called a meeting of the animals and told them of his plan. 'Suppose,' said the jackal, 'we promised to

239

send one animal every day for the tiger's dinner. Then the rest of us would be safe that day, for he would not go roaring through the forest killing everyone he met.' (And the jackal thought in his cunning head, 'We could send all the small animals first, and then *I* should be safe for a very long time.')

The other animals agreed. The tiger agreed. He was growing fat and lazy, and it saved him trouble. Everyone was pleased except the little hare. When they told him he was to run along and be the tiger's dinner, he was not pleased at all. And I really do not wonder – do you?

So now you know why everyone in the forest was so worried that beautiful sunshiny morning. The animals were all afraid that if the tiger was kept waiting for his dinner he might come to fetch it and perhaps fetch several of them as well.

But nobody could persuade the little hare to go, and nobody wanted to go instead of him. The sun crept up and up the sky till it was shining just overhead, which meant it was twelve o'clock. All the little hare would say when they told him how badly he was behaving, was, 'Don't disturb me; I am thinking.' And by this time the tiger could plainly be heard roaring with rage, but luckily he was too fat and lazy to trouble to leave his den.

However, twelve o'clock in the forest is a hot and sleepy time of day. Presently the tiger was quiet; even the jackal stopped talking, and most of the animals were having a little midday nap. So they were all very much surprised when, just as the shadows of the rocks and trees had grown large enough to show that it was one o'clock, the little hare suddenly gave a jump and a shout. 'I'm off,' he said. And off he went, running so fast that it really seemed as if he would fall head over heels. And when the animals saw which way he was running they all gave

a great sigh, or a squeak, or a grunt of relief, and began to look about to see what they could find for their dinners.

Where do you think the little hare was going? You will be very surprised to hear that he ran straight to the cave where the tiger lived. He was in such a hurry that when he got there it seemed as if he couldn't stop himself, and he almost tumbled into the tiger's paws. But not quite into them; he was very careful to keep just out of reach. The tiger was very angry at having been kept waiting so long, but he had been dozing and was still only half awake. So instead of putting out his big paw to catch the little hare, he growled, 'Come here, you miserable little creature, and don't tumble about like that. What do you mean by being so late?'

The little hare began to sob. (He was panting so much that it was easy to pretend.) 'Oh, my lord tiger,' he said, 'I am so thin, so very thin, and my brother was so fat.'

'Then why didn't they send him instead?' roared the tiger.

'They did,' said the little hare; 'they did. Oh, they did. But the other tiger got him first.'

'Who-oo-oo-oo-oo?' roared the tiger.

'The other tiger,' sobbed the little hare, 'who lives in the hole among the bushes near by.'

'Take me to him,' roared the tiger; 'I will teach him to eat my dinner and leave a miserable thing like you.'

'Very well,' said the little hare, still sobbing. 'Very well. Come this way, my lord. Come quietly, and I will take you to his den.'

And the little hare led the tiger to a narrow path which wound in and out among the tall grass. Tigers are like cats, they cannot see very well in the bright sunlight, and the tiger blinked and peered this way and that. Suddenly the little hare darted into some bushes. 'This way, my lord,' he said, 'this way.' The tiger leaped over the bushes and landed in a little open space. There was a deep hole, by the side of which stood the little hare. 'Here is his den, my lord,' he said, in a trembling voice. 'Oh! oh! oh! I am so frightened. Let me stand close beside you!'

The tiger went to the edge and looked. There, looking up at him out of the hole, was the face of a very angry tiger, and beside him was a very frightened hare.

'*Give me my dinner,*' roared the tiger, and he jumped – and splash! he went, down and down and down. And he never came up any more. For the hole was a deep well, filled with water as clear and shining as a looking-glass, and the tiger with whom he was so angry was really his greedy self with the little hare at his side.

As for the little hare, he went scampering back to the open space where this story begins. And there he found a hollow log and climbed upon it, and he drummed with his strong hind legs and sang:

> 'Come! Come! Come!
> I beat upon the drum.
> Pr-r-rump, pr-r-rump, pr-r-rump,
> I saw the tiger jump.
> Down in the well he fell,
> As I am here to tell.
> Pr-r-rump, pr-r-rump, pr-r-rump,
> I saw the tiger jump!'

The animals came creeping out of the bushes to listen, and when the little hare had sung it all through, they all joined in and sang joyfully in chorus:

> 'Down in the well he fell:
> The hare is here to tell.'

till they were all quite hoarse with singing. And then they all went happily home to sleep.

From *More Stories and How to Tell Them*

Cross-Patch

BY MARGARET BAKER

There was once a little woman and her name was Betsy Cross-Patch. She was so very bad-tempered that she could not shut the door without slamming it, nor put a cup and saucer on the table without making them rattle; and she never spoke without scolding and complaining.

At last the door grew tired of being slammed. 'It's not fair,' he said to the chimney. 'I'm a well-made, well-behaved door, but she's always grumbling about me. She shall have some reason for grumbling in future – I am going to stick!'

'Have you heard about the door?' the chimney asked the pan. 'He's tired of the little woman's grumblings and he's going to stick every time she tries to open him.'

'You don't say so!' exclaimed the pan.

'Indeed I do,' said the chimney; 'and what is more, I am tired of her complaints myself. No matter how well I draw she always has some fault to find, so why should I bother to do my

work properly? In future I'm going to smoke every time she lights the fire.'

'Have you heard about the door and the chimney?' the pan asked the chair. 'They are so tired of being scolded for no reason at all, that the door is going to stick and the chimney to smoke.'

'Well, to be sure!' cried the chair.

'I think it is a very good idea and I mean to copy it,' said the pan. 'However hard I try to please her I cannot cook anything to her liking, so I intend to boil over every time she puts me on the fire.'

'I think I shall follow your example myself,' said the chair. 'If the door is going to stick, and the chimney is going to smoke, and you are going to boil over, I don't see why I shouldn't overbalance.'

Now the little woman had been to market that day. All the way there she grumbled that the sun was too hot and the wind was too cold and the road was too dusty, and she never once looked up to see how pretty the hedges looked in their fresh green leaves, nor to laugh at the lambs skipping and racing in the fields. All the time she was at the market she was grumbling that there was nothing worth buying and that everything cost too much, and she never once stopped for a chat with any of the people who said 'Good day' to her. And all the way home she was grumbling that the way was too long and her basket was too heavy, and she was grumbling so loudly that she never heard Farmer Turniptop offer her a lift in his cart.

'I don't see why other people should have such an easy life, while everything goes wrong for me!' she complained.

When she reached home she jerked the string that pulled up the latch and tried to push the door open.

But the door stuck!

'What can be the matter with it?' she cried. 'It has always been a very good door before.'

'Then why did you grumble about me?' asked the door, and opened so suddenly that the little old woman nearly fell over the sill.

She put her basket down with a thump and snatched up the bellows to blow the fire, for she was very hungry after her walk and wanted to cook her dinner. But no sooner had the flames begun to curl up the chimney, than the chimney began to smoke.

It smoked and it smoked till the little woman thought her head would waggle off with sneezing and coughing.

'What can be the matter with it?' she gasped. 'It was always a very good chimney before!'

'Then why did you grumble about me?' asked the chimney.

She hurried to the shelf, took down the pan, filled it with broth and put it on the fire, for so much coughing and sneezing made her hungrier than ever; but hardly was her back turned than the pot boiled over.

'Oh dear; Oh dear!' she cried. 'And it was always such a good pan before!'

'Then I can't think why you complained so much about me,' said the pan.

By this time the little woman was feeling very tired: she sat down in the chair to rest, but the chair overbalanced and tumbled her on to the floor!

'Lawks-a-mussey-me!' cried the little woman. 'It has been such a steady, comfortable chair. Why should it play tricks like this! I must be bewitched!'

'Not a bit of it,' said the chair; 'but as you always grumbled whatever we did, we thought we might as well deserve the unkind things you said about us. I'm sure I don't like over-balancing, and if you'll treat me fairly I'll never do it again.'

'It's no pleasure to *me* to boil over,' said the pan.

'I *hate* smoking,' said the chimney.

'And I can't *bear* sticking,' said the door, 'but you can't get the best, even out of a door, if you're always finding fault, you know.'

The little woman was so surprised that she could not think of a word to say for ever so long. She sat on the floor just where she had tumbled and thought the most surprising thoughts. Then she got to her feet. First she picked up the chair and put it in its place; then she set the pan carefully on the hob, poked the fire gently, and shut the door without slamming it.

'Fair is fair,' she said, 'and I've only got what I deserve. If I want treating pleasantly I'll have to behave pleasantly myself.'

So the little woman stopped grumbling, and after that the door never stuck, and the chimney never smoked, and the pan never boiled over, and the chair never overbalanced, and they all lived comfortably together for always and always.

From *Tell Them Again Tales*

The Train to Glasgow

Here is the train to Glasgow.

Here is the driver,
Mr MacIver,
Who drove the train to Glasgow.

Here is the guard from Donibristle
Who waved his flag and blew his whistle
To tell the driver,
Mr MacIver,
To start the train to Glasgow.

Here is a boy called Donald MacBrain
Who came to the station to catch the train
But saw the guard from Donibristle
Wave his flag and blow his whistle
To tell the driver,
Mr MacIver,
To start the train to Glasgow.

Here is the guard, a kindly man
Who at the last moment, hauled into the van
That fortunate boy called Donald MacBrain
Who came to the station to catch the train
But saw the guard from Donibristle
Wave his flag and blow his whistle

To tell the driver,
Mr MacIver,
To start the train to Glasgow.

Here are the hens and here are the cocks
Clucking and crowing inside a box,
In charge of the guard, that kindly man
Who at the last moment, hauled into the van
That fortunate boy called Donald MacBrain
Who came to the station to catch the train
But saw the guard from Donibristle
Wave his flag and blow his whistle
To tell the driver,
Mr MacIver,
To start the train to Glasgow.

Here is the train. It gave a jolt
Which loosened a catch and loosened a bolt,
And let out the hens and let out the cocks
Clucking and crowing out of their box,
In charge of the guard, that kindly man
Who at the last moment, hauled into the van
That fortunate boy called Donald MacBrain
Who came to the station to catch the train
But saw the guard from Donibristle
Wave his flag and blow his whistle
To tell the driver,
Mr MacIver,
To start the train to Glasgow.

The guard chased a hen and, missing it, fell.
The hens were all squawking, the cocks were as well,
And unless you were there you haven't a notion
The flurry, the fuss, the noise and commotion
Caused by the train which gave a jolt
And loosened a catch and loosened a bolt,
And let out the hens and let out the cocks
Clucking and crowing out of their box,
In charge of the guard, that kindly man
Who at the last moment, hauled into the van
That fortunate boy called Donald MacBrain
Who came to the station to catch the train
But saw the guard from Donibristle
Wave his flag and blow his whistle
To tell the driver,
Mr MacIver,
To start the train to Glasgow.

TELL ME ANOTHER STORY

Now Donald was quick and Donald was neat
And Donald was nimble on his feet.
He caught the hens and he caught the cocks
And he put them back in their great big box.
The guard was pleased as pleased could be
And invited Donald to come to tea
On Saturday, at Donibristle,
And let him blow his lovely whistle,
And said in all his life he'd never
Seen a boy so quick and clever,
And so did the driver,
Mr MacIver,
Who drove the train to Glasgow.

WILMA HORSBROUGH From *Clinkerdump*

Stories for Under-fives
Stories for Five-year-olds
Stories for Six-year-olds
Stories for Seven-year-olds
More Stories for Seven-year-olds
Stories for Eight-year-olds
Stories for Nine-year-olds
Stories for Tens and over *ed. Sara and Stephen Corrin*

Beautifully chosen collections of superb stories, which have been carefully graded to suit the developing interests and imaginations of the different age groups.

The Dead Letter Box *Jan Mark*

Louie's friend Glenda moves house and Louise arranges a 'dead' letter box in a book in the library. Unfortunately, Glenda is no letter writer and the end result is chaos in the library!

Two Village Dinosaurs *Phyllis Arkle*

Two dinosaurs spell double trouble as Dino and Sauro trample their amiable way through the village, causing chaos and confusion on every side.

Casey the Utterly Impossible Horse *Anita Feagles*

Mike finds a horse who wants to live in the garage, but it wants to be called Mike too, or failing that, Kitty Cat. And it keeps demanding awkward things like party invitations and striped pyjamas, creating all sorts of problems!

Changing of the Guard and Wallpaper Holiday *H. E. Todd*

Two delightful stories for reading aloud or for readers of seven and over.

The House that Moved *David Rees*

Adam and Donald had used the derelict old house for ages as their own secret place. So when the council decided to move it to make way for a new road, Adam and Donald were determined to get involved. But nobody could have guessed just how involved they were going to get!

Dinner at Alberta's *Russell Hoban*

Arthur the crocodile has extremely bad table manners — until he is invited to dinner at Alberta's.

A Walk Down the Pier *John Escott*

When part of the pier drops into the sea, Davy is in a dilemma — how can he get help for Mr Pennyquick, who lies injured in the pavilion at the end of the pier?